For my darling wife, my beautiful children

and all lovers of the Ian Fleming's masterpiece

LIVE TODAY,

DIE TOMORROW

7

Orbis non sufficit

Chapter I

The Beginning

Fettes College, Edinburgh.

'Bloody pleb! They let any scum in nowadays.' Came the usual malicious taunt as he was roughly pushed aside as he made his way towards the imposing gothic main building. His shoulder stinging from the sharp impact against the solid face of the newly erected Hazeldean Sandstone wall of the new neighbouring Spens Building. He exhaled deeply remembering what his uncle Max had taught him. *"Arm yourself with a thick skin. Take no notice of them, simple words cannot hurt you."* He used to tell him.

He had witnessed this direct classist victimisation all before during his brief time at Eton before he was formally expelled for a brief and somewhat casual adolescent dalliance with one of the young foreign females of the Colleges cleaning team. Although he had protested his innocence to the college's Head, who had always shown a blatant negative bias towards him had already deregistered him and informed his responsible adults, his aunt and uncle of the dishonourable act and that they could be expecting him home before the week was out.

It transpired that his new Head Dean had a similar ethos of unfrequented dislike to him and this had ensured his welcome to Fettes was not a joyous one the previous year. When he first started at Fettes the archaic and customary traditions of *bothering* soon became apparent as the children of the senior ilk, all prodigals of Oxbridge elites no less. Tested the waters with the smallest new boys, or "New Bloods" as they called them. Similar in fashion to those barbaric fox hunters the older hunt masters, in this case the seniors, would initiate the younger year of aggressors by wiping the blood of their first victim on their cheek and forehead. The act of blooding was truly traumatising. Their desire to humiliate and taunt their prey until they either fought back (which was utterly hopeless and demeaning) or they simply broke down into tears to then be scared and ashamed to live out their remaining years trembling with trepidation as they awaited the next instalment. Either result was welcomed by these obstinate brutes, but the latter was their genuine goal, to see those beneath them squirm and flinch as they literally lorded over them as they strut throughout the grounds.

And the day had finally come for him to enter their roaming crosshair, as the *New Blood* to be tested. Seven against one, bad odds to anyone but to arrogant elitist bullies this was fair bloodsport.

"*Nature*" they had called it. Darwin's theory of strength through evolution in practical representation. Their harsh and barbaric Spartan ethos frequently found in British boarding establishments resulted in the unhealthy removal of sympathy, kindness and basic human respect for equality. This explained a lot about the British politician mentality of self-preservation at the expense of millions of unknowing citizens who found themselves victims of an unjust callous system led by spoiled ruthless sociopathic tyrants.

Eton College had been the same of course but he'd evaded direct engagement by joining the rugby team. Much like any athletic fraternity, if you mess with one member of the team you'd soon find the rest of the team waiting for you to exact revenge, but not at Fettes. Here he was deemed too small, diminutive and weedy to join their superiorist band of colossal teens. It was undeniable that although he was tall for his age, some would even suggest above average for most teens his peerage. And although he was of a strong but wiry build he topped most of his class peer's by several inches, but the senior years were a different breed altogether. Some of them already stood well over six feet tall and physically primed for a professional career in rugby or Pro-wrestling.

But size, he knew, was not always an advantage and being a clear foot shorter than them could be something he could use against them. He rubbed the ache out of his bruised shoulder as he once more heard his uncle Max's voice from within his mind quoting the line from his favourite novel, The Power of One by Bryce Courtney, *"Little beats big when little is smart, first with the head, then with the heart."*

Much akin to the novel's main protagonist 'PK' he too had learnt to defend himself from a young age. Having been taught the art of Jujitsu when he was six years old, he had progressed swiftly to a Green Belt, the highest he could go as a minor. He had travelled a lot with his parents before the accident, and as they socialised and attended a multitude of business dinners, he had kept himself hidden away on those endless nights in the throngs of hotels throughout Europe watching thousands of YouTube videos on MMA (Mixed-Martial-Arts), on home-schooled self-defence and techniques usually reserved for those in special forces. Being a single child he didn't partake in playful scuffles as most young boys do. But his uncle Max, an ex-special forces combat trainer had told him to never show your weakness. *"They are like starved wolves… once they see vulnerability, they will never leave you be."* He had never been one to back away from a fight and he certainly knew how to handle himself. Although he held himself with a confidence that would normally deter this sort of insensitive nonsense, he finally realised that these subjugators really didn't know him and to them he was just their next victim.

The day had started with the typical name calling, which he had heard used on others in the previous months. His oppressors never missed an opportunity to disparage him with bespoke malignant torrents insulting his Middle-Class background, and his casual and apparent common appearance. The boys had even managed to turn the majority of his peers against him, ensuring that they always made a comment about his personal hygiene, stating that they could smell how poor he was as he walked past. Or they would hold their noses as he neared or passed through a corridor. This was one thing that he really didn't comprehend as his was probably the best personal hygiene in the entire school. They loved provoking the fact that his uncle funded his tuition at the College, something they found immensely amusing. All of which he ignored, held his chin high and proud as he continued to walk away. He believed if he did not rise to their taunts, they would become bored and swiftly move on to new prey. But today his gut told him that this wasn't going to work, something was different. He held his tongue and kept his stare firm as he took their elbow strikes as he carried on past them.

For the younger years this common assault became a daily occurrence as they moved around the school. He didn't really care what they said, it hurt him of course, but he was told to never let them see you weak or crying. Something that was hard to resist when some of these bastards had really bony elbows. *"Clear your mind"* he told himself. *"Only a week to go."*

He focused on his life away from college; he had spent the last three years in the care of his Aunt Charmian and Uncle Max in a small town called Pett Bottom. They had become his legal guardians shortly after his eleventh birthday following the tragic death of both of his parents after a mountain-climbing accident in Aiguilles Rouges near Chamonix.

His aunt doted on him having no children of their own and his uncle tried his hardest to toughen him up for the world. His uncle was nothing like his late father, who had been a travelling representative for an armaments company based in Europe. His uncle had chosen to join the commandos and later the special forces instead. Both used to jest their careers were cutthroat, which as a young boy he never really understood.

He had endured the first year at Fettes mostly in solitude given the fact that he was favourably being avoided by his peers due to their own fears of hostility from the bullies either by association or simply by perception of being nice to him. He had grown to like his own company, but he longed to return home to his aunt and uncle in the south of Canterbury, Kent. He had even contemplated returning to his family home in Glen Coe, Scotland for the summer, this is a place he had not returned to since his parents passed away three years before. It had always held a bitter taste in his mouth and sharp pain in his stomach whenever he thought of it.

Four days remained until he would be free of the tyrants, but this day was different. This day their leader, Quentin Campbell, the personification of a public-school douchebag, didn't make a single comment as he approached. Instead, he waited for his six large friends to stand awkwardly in anticipation for the torrent of insults or pithy comments on his fictional body odour or necessitous upbringing. But none came. Instead, he stood with a half-smile as he pulled out a sheet of paper and began reading out the words written within.

'Dear Mr Grant, I write to you with a heavy heart.' Campbell started not looking up but smiling broadly.

"Shit!" he said to himself. He still didn't react, but he knew full well what was coming.

'The sale of the Skyfall estate in Glen Coe has fallen through, and we will be unable to pay for next year's tuition at this time.' He laughed as he read aloud, 'I must ask that you are charitable and allow me more time to find the boarders fees for September.'

'Begging for charity, you really are a pleb.' Spat one of the tormentors' inches from his face.

'You will understand…' Campbell continued to read, 'That following the demise of his parents, he will not be able to access his inheritance until his eighteenth birthday.'

'Bloody Pov!' Shouted another of the posse aggressively, spitting in his face as another jabbed him in the arm.

'Is this why they threw you out of Eton, you smelly little urchin.' Cried another jeering and laughing in his face. 'Because you couldn't pay your fees?'

'It looks like you will be leaving us next term if your scumbag pleb uncle can't raise the money, but we haven't finished with you yet.' Sneered Campbell, his eyes wide and excited. 'So, we need to remedy this before you go off to an orphan ridden council estate Academy school in some dirty little pleb town.' He said screwing up the letter in his hand before throwing it to the floor.

'No one loves you?' Mocked Campbell smugly as his friends jeered him on. 'Because your poor mummy and daddy are dead!' He spat, nodding to his entourage who all laughed.

He exhaled hard but remained silent, his eyes taking in each malicious gesture and laughing face surrounding him. His ears picked up every hurtful word being said as the amassed pupils began to laugh and jeer. He turned to see one of the other boys had been recording the incident on his mobile phone, he assumed that their intention was to post it online to further ridicule him by violating his dignity to the wider world.

'No wonder his uncle got rid of him, the smelly Pov bastard!' jeered one of the boys from behind him, 'But he should know better than to send poor stinking scum into our school.'

He winced as one of the boys stood behind pulled his scruffy blonde hair back lifting his chin as another ran in to punch him hard in the stomach making him double over as they pushed him to the floor so that he lay flat on his stomach, he could hear them urging each other on to kick him whilst he was down. His tormentors had now taken it to the next level. The level that his uncle Max had always told him, he could retaliate against. *'Finally'*.

He rolled over to see the boy with the phone had carelessly moved in to better see his face, staring at the screen instead of down to the floor where he lay. A very common and rather stupid occurrence where people don't seem to realise, they need to be vigilant of their surroundings, and not transfixed to a digital screen. He saw his opportunity and kicked hard to the side of the videoing boy's knee with his heel sending him down in a scream of agonising pain. Whilst still on the ground he quickly grabbed another by the leg, placing his knee over their toes holding them fast and flat to the ground he forcefully pushed the boy back causing their ankle to tear with a brutal popping sound.

He jumped up as the others raced in to unleash their assault upon him. He blocked several punches, but they moved fast. Their larger bodies and longer arms managed to restrain him one on each limb, holding him steady as Campbell started a volley of blows to his face. The impact of Campbell's large fists shook him throughout, his head fizzing and his stomach tingling as his body filled with adrenaline. That uncontrollable sensation that fills you making every atom of your body shake as your stomach fills with nausea similar to when you are falling. He struggled with his captors until one of Campbell's blows missed his face and hit one of his companions, resulting in them loosening their tight grip on his arm. Using this to his advantage he punched the boy hard in the throat sending him wheezing to his knees. He grabbed the face of another pushing his thumb hard into the left eye socket until the boy let go of his other arm, screaming in agony they took two paces back. Another opportunity opened before him as he moved in on the semi-blinded attacker. A smooth combination of four punches sent the larger boy to the floor.

'Three left' he said, wiping his bloodied nose as Campbell backed off.

'Well get him then!' Shouted Campbell anxiously to the two remaining bullies who looked at each other hesitantly.

The larger of the two boys ran at him with a haymaker swinging his arm around for momentum which when done properly can be devastating. But this also shows your opponent exactly what you plan to do leaving you open. The large boy came in for the punch roaring wildly as he swung.

With a swift dodge to the side the large boy continued past into the gathered pupils sending them all flying. He struck the now prone boy in the back of the neck with a hard slap dropping his limp body down hard to the floor.

The last boy adopted a classic pugilist boxer's stance, his fists raised guarding his face and upper body, his head ducked down his chin in his chest. He stepped in jabbing left and right, the punches were hard and fast.

"*He knows what he's doing*" he said to himself as he mirrored the larger boy's stance.

They exchanged multiple jabs and blows, but the larger boy's reach was easily a foot longer than his. The fight took him back for a second to when he used to spar with his father when they had been on holiday in Switzerland visiting his mother's family in Canton de Vaud.

A straight jab to the forehead brought him swiftly back into the real world as the attacker swung again. He didn't blink but instead moved quickly into the attacker's punch raising his elbow to stop the punch and force it upwards. He then threw a devastating uppercut to the boy's jaw followed very quickly with an elbow to the same spot. Then a heavy right hook to the boy's left temple. The boy's head wobbled as his eyes dilated, his gaze fuzzy and lost. Falling spreadeagled to the floor the boy began snoring heavily and rapidly. Completely unconscious.

He shook his aching fists and gathered his composure taking in several deep breaths. He looked to the ground at the six incapacitate boys now crying, screaming or unconscious on the floor. The groups of spectators began clapping as he wiped his hand on his scuffed and torn maroon uniform blazer. 'Your turn now Campbell.' He said quietly. 'Just you.'

'Fine…' retorted Campbell sourly as he edged forward, 'I'll take care of you myself!' he roared in frustration.

'Come on Campbell.' He said irritably, gesturing him closer with his fingers. 'Let's finish this.'

'You see what happens when they let stinking Middle-Class chavs into our schools.' Spat Campbell.

Campbell was more than thirty kilograms heavier than him and easily a foot taller, but he was an amateur at fighting one on one. His normal modus operandi of attack ordinarily involves six or more others to act for him to aid in his assault. Campbell threw three wild punches, lunging and overreaching with each throw. As the fourth punch came the bruised but ready boy made his move, he blocked it easily with his left elbow and grabbed Campbell's outstretched arm by the wrist. He twisted it out sharply at an angle to put pressure on the Extensor tendons making Campbell bend slightly at the knee as he released a volley of five precise and extremely hard punches to Campbells pretty face striking hard at the ridge of his already large nose, hitting the same spot with each punch. His knuckles screamed with each impact, but it felt surprisingly pleasing. He finished with a swift upward kick to Campbell's groin that lifted him off the ground. Campbell took several steps back before falling on his arse, his eyes wet with tears and his nose spurting violently with fresh red blood all over his chin and maroon uniform.

'How is the smell now Campbell?' He smiled, shaking his aching fists.

'You wait until my father hears about this you dirty Pov bastard!' shouted a crestfallen Campbell through bloodied teeth as he tried to stem the torrent of blood flowing from his devastated nose.

The victorious boy turned defiantly to a student who had also been recording the incident on his mobile phone and raised an eyebrow. He ushered for the boy to hand it over to him which he did without quibble. 'Next time, try helping your fellow man instead of silently spectating. You will go further in life that way.' He quickly deleted the video and dropped it back into the ashen faced student's hand.

He set to picking up his school satchel from the ground and went to collect some other items from the ground around him when a loud authoritative voice bellowed from behind him.

'Nobody moves a bloody muscle!' shouted the voice of Mr McGee the vice Dean of Fettes College. One of the most imposing and feared teachers on the campus, his archaic and outdated abusive methods were questionable at best. One of those stalwart dinosaurs who still believed the pupils should be caned every day to ensure continued discipline regardless of the severity of their misdemeanours.

His long gown billowed as he wafted determinedly towards the gathered group of students, 'Right!' he shouted, 'Who started this?' he continued as he parted several pupils with his long sleeved arms so he could better see the cause for such a commotion.

'Another tussle at school, boy? I thought you'd be bored of being sent to see the Head…' he grabbed the boy by the ear and pushed him forward, 'Come on, off with you now.' He looked back to the seven senior pupils still nursing their wounds on the floor, his eyebrow raised. 'Bested by a second year no less….' He muttered indignantly as he forcibly pulled them up by their scruffs and back onto their feet. 'You should all be ashamed of yourselves.' He shook his head disapprovingly then looked back to the second year as he disappeared around a corner out of sight. 'He really did a number on you all.' He smiled sadistically.

The undefeated and triumphant boy slunked away from the gathering towards the Head Dean's office as he let out a half-smile. He hurt all over, but he was impressed by his achievements. Although this time he was certain the Head would expel him without any hesitation. He cleared the corner and waited until he was well out of sight when he pulled his hand out to reveal two stolen mobile phones and three wallets from his fallen and dishevelled attackers. He was no petty thief but for what he had planned he had to play his cards when they were dealt in his favour. "*Being an opportunist could get you out of many a dire situation,*" this was another of his uncle Max's favourite sayings.

He approached the Head Dean's office door and gave a hesitant knock with his bruised knuckles as he closed an App on one of the looted phones and slipped it back into his pocket.

'Come!' bellowed the broad Scottish voice from within. The boy entered sheepishly and went to stand behind the large teak writing desk, behind which was stood an old wizened man in long black robes. The man was in his late sixties with a scruffy grey side parting hopelessly trying to hide the balding scalp beneath, he wore thick horn-rimmed glasses attached with a beaded chain around his dandruff covered neck and shoulders. He gave a half-glance at the boy as he continued staring out of one of the large bay windows to the vast college grounds outside.

'Sir,' started the boy with a little bow.

'Well, what is it this time boy?' snapped the old man indignantly. His strong Scottish accent filled the otherwise silent room.

'A fight Sir…' replied the boy timidly. The old man turned to eye him up and down then returned to gaze out of the window.

'Seldom do we have so much trouble from one student.' Snapped the man again. 'You will never make anything of yourself if you continue to behave like this laddie.' The old man walked over to his desk moving some papers aside as though searching for something. 'I was going to send for you anyway, I received a letter from your uncle today, boy.'

'Yes Sir, I know Sir.' Replied the boy quietly.

'Do you now laddie?' he eyed him over his horn-rimmed glasses as he again scanned the desk's unkempt surface. 'Then you will be aware that we will not be having you back after the summer break.' He started, 'We at Fettes are not a charity! For one hundred and fifty years we have prided ourselves on our privileged educational programmes. These past twelve months you have shown us that you are as smart and resourceful as the other children here. But you have done nothing but cause me distress and concern with this continued anti-social behaviour. How many times has it been now boy? How many times have you stood before me… afore my desk with that pathetic look upon your face?' The boy stood in silence and looked to the ground; he kicked his feet as the old man spoke. 'You've a smart head upon your wee shoulders and you're mature for your age laddie… You act like a man… a damned foolish one but a man none-the-less. You have gumption and a good heart… Much like your father when he was here… But not even his consequential favour is going to save you this time.' The young boy looked up at the mention of his father. He knew his father had studied here years before, but none of the staff were old enough to remember, none except the ancient Head Dean. 'Your father was a fine student, top of his class and captain of near enough every team we had going. In this instance I can honestly and disappointingly say the apple didn't fall close enough.' He paced as he spoke, squinting occasionally out of the large antique came rimmed bay windows. 'So, laddie… This fight of yours. Who was involved?'

'Quentin Campbell Sir… And six of his friends.' Replied the boy solemnly rubbing his reddened knuckles.

'Campbell, the captain of the rugby team?' he repeated looking the boy up and down. 'Aye, you do look rather battered. 'No doubt a one sided affair but nonetheless, this is the final straw, my boy. No more free passes… D'you understand what this means laddie?' The boy stood silent; head bowed in submission. 'D'You have anything to say for yourself laddie?' said the old man, his face finally showing a glimpse of sympathy.

'I accept responsibility for my actions, as I was raised to do.' replied the boy proudly.

'No doubt…' He tapped the desk with his hand impatiently. 'Well, there you are then. You can say goodbye to your friends whilst you gather your belongings from your dormitory and wait in the reception. I will call your uncle to collect you this evening.'

'Thank you, Sir,' started the boy, his cold grey eyes now fixed on the old man. He went to say something else when one of the phones in his pocket pinged loudly making him pause. The Head Dean shook his head frustratedly, 'You know the motto of this college boy?' said the old man now leaning heavily on his desk. "*Industria*" He said wholesomely with a wee nod. 'Meaning industry, labour and diligence… that is what makes you ready to conquer this world boy.'

'And what if the world is not enough Sir?' replied the boy seriously.

The Head looked him up and down again but said nothing. He was about to challenge him for his cheek and impudence but instead raised an eyebrow, 'What do you mean by that wee comment?'

'Do you ever think that…' he started before watching the old man's eyes, that look of annoyance and impatience, 'Nothing Sir.' He trailed off. 'Good bye Sir.'

The old man waved him away with a nonchalant back hand as he turned walking back to his bay window, banging heavily on the glass shaking his finger indignantly at a young student who was running along the path outside.

The boy slipped out of the office without looking back and made his way to his dormitory where he began collecting his few belongings. He placed some items into his satchel and others into a large waterproof hiking backpack that his uncle had given him for his last birthday. He was not sure when the occasion would have called for him to use it whilst at the college but for now, he was glad to have it. All of his large textbooks and other school items he left on one of the writing desks in the dorm. He would not need them where he was heading, and they would have slowed him down. He looked one last time and smiled broadly, for the first time in a long time he was actually happy. Another pupil walked in as he was leaving and although they had shared the dormitory for the past twelve months, they had never really spoken other than exchanging formalities and a simple hello.

"Good show with Campbell… He will not live that one down for a while. Are you really going then?' asked the boy a little awkwardly.

'Well of course I am… People like me are destined for greater things.' he replied with a smile and walked away without another word.

The boy swiftly made his way to the groundskeeper's storeroom where he entered without knocking. Inside was a burly ginger man in his forties with a thick tangled beard and dark beanie hat pulled down behind his ears making them protrude comically. He was dressed in an old blue overall that was more oil and grease than fabric, his dishevelled appearance making him look more like a vagrant than a groundskeeper. The large man nodded while wrestling with an oily chain saw on his workbench. The man simply oozed a languid approach to his groundskeepers duties, it was a miracle any work was done at all.

'Hello Mack,' started the boy shaking the man's dirty hand. 'I'm leaving the college now… permanently. I just wanted to say thank you… for being someone to talk to.'

'Oh aye, right you are…' said the groundskeeper with a nod taking his preferred hand giving it a wee shake. 'I know these places can be hard for wee ones, away from their mammies and daddies for so long. I have seen many a kid gettin up tight or losing it. I was told to always help someone, because you may be the only one that does.'

The boy nodded in agreement, 'Wise words.'

'Of course they are… They are mine.' laughed the groundskeeper, exposing several gold teeth. He clicked a finger dropping the chainsaw. 'Oh, your wee Amazon package arrived this morning by the way. You'll be wanting it now, I suppose?' he asked, picking it up and handing it over to him. 'It's bloody heavy you ken… I never ask what you order but this one has me intrigued.'

The boy took hold of the heavy delivery package and smiled. 'Fishing magnets… For my new project.' he replied honestly.

'Aye, a fine hobby fishing, you know I once caught a-' he started as one of the phones in the boy's pocket pinged loudly again.

'Sorry Mack, I have got to run. Thank you again.' he said sincerely, shouldering his satchel and backpack.

'Guidbye Bye Bye for noo See ye efter, kidda.' Smiled Mack through his large beard.

Chapter II

The Journey Begins

A1 Southbound

The boy stood patiently on Carrington Road at the junction with Fettes Avenue looking over to the sports pitches across the road. The college encompassed a huge area of nearly 300 acres and consisted of swimming pools, shooting range, athletics tracks, golf course, woodlands and multiple specialist buildings. He wouldn't miss any of them. Turning to have a final look at the large maroon sign that read '*Fettes College*' bolted onto the black iron gates at the end of the long driveway he exhaled heavily. "*Good bye and good riddance*" he muttered to himself.

On the far end of the drive, he took in the infamous gothic silhouette of the old house's spires standing prominently visible on the horizon. This was a sight he would not be missing. He turned at the sound of an approaching vehicle as he gave a small wave as a black Mercedes V-Class MPV rolled to a stop in front of him as the tinted window silently lowered revealing a young Indian man behind the wheel. 'You order an Uber mate?' his accent unmistakably local.

'That I did.' Smiled the boy as he took off his backpack and satchel and opened the rear driver side door.

'Now I just want to check with you before we go anywhere. You want to go from Edinburgh to Hull, that is two hundred and sixty miles…' said the driver quizzically.

'Yes.' Replied the boy with a smile.

'That is going to take at least six hours, then I have to come all the way back again.'

'Yes…' he replied, still smiling, 'That is your chosen occupation isn't it… to drive people around?'

'Alright, no need to be rude about it… I was just checking is all.' Retorted the driver.

'Apologies, look I'll tell you what, pull over in town by the nearest cashpoint and I will give you £300 extra for your trouble.'

'You know we can't take extra money from customers?' replied the driver stubbornly.

'Well let's call it a donation then.' He said sliding the door shut as he clicked on his seatbelt as the Mercedes pulled away.

He had always been observant and noticed the little things that others never really paid attention to. During school outings or trips into town he had always observed his peers (especially his tormentors) entering their passwords or pins into their mobile phones, another trick he had discovered was that he could remember things remarkably well. He removed the two "borrowed" mobile telephones and to his astonishment and gratitude, it also transpired that his abusive peers each used banking apps that allowed them to change their pin numbers by the press of a button, which allowed him complete unadulterated access to their money. And there was no denying that these elitist families were stupendously well off.

Five minutes later he climbed out of the MPV and slipped off his maroon school blazer, throwing it into a nearby dustbin. He smiled broadly as he pulled on his trusty grey hoodie pulling it up over his bruised face. Slipping two pieces of chewing gum into his mouth he walked across to the RBS cashpoint beside the small convenience store in suburban Edinburgh. He approached from the side keeping his head down, his hood covering his face completely. He raised an arm and placed it over the small, convex mirrored disk at the top centre of the cash point. Using his other hand, he removed the gum from his mouth and quickly smeared it over the mirrored disk. Now with both hands free he began inserting each of the plethora of stolen bank cards maxing out all of them, withdrawing as much as each would allow him, £500 from each of Campbells which made him smile. 'Karmas a bitch.' He laughed aloud, pocketing his well earned money. You don't need to be a genius to know that as soon as the cards had been reported as stolen the banks would block them and make them useless. Then the banks would make enquires as to when and where they had been used, asking for the date, time and exact amount of the transaction to start the slow and laborious police reports process. This he didn't worry about, safe in the knowledge that his identity was unknown thanks to a little initiative and some basic chewing gum placed over the units only CCTV feed.

True to his word he did indeed hand over the extra £300 to the Uber driver as they set off along the A1 southbound to his next destination. Having access to his own moderate savings-account he had never wanted for anything. His family had also always been well off, but since his parents had died three years previous his uncle and aunt had supported him financially as the family inheritance and rather hefty life insurance policies both his parents had in place were locked by the Royal Bank of Scotland until his eighteenth birthday. He would only be fifteen on the 11th November, that is why he had decided to act like a small-time criminal and teach his abusers a lesson, plus the extra money would be very beneficial for what he was planning.

During the Uber ride the boy sat in absolute silence searching the internet on his own mobile phone to finalise his preparations and look up the scuba centre from his saved bookmarks. The shopping basket had already been filled with everything he would need for his journey. He was more than hesitant on using one of his own bank cards for the purchase of the kit so he sent a message to the company of his scheduled arrival later that evening and that he would be paying in cash.

'Look, do you mind if we stop at a McDonald's when we reach Newcastle-upon-Tyne, the one by the ferry port?' He asked the driver.

'Whatever you want, boss.' Replied the driver.

'Excellent, I am going to get some sleep, I'm exhausted. Please wake me when we arrive.'

The driver turned down the radio and nodded to himself as the boy turned over to sleep in the back, he put his hand into his jacket pocket removing the £300 cash and smiled broadly to himself.

The boy was gently woken by the driver as he looked out of the car window to see a large DFDS Newcastle sign pointing off to their left. The two and a half hours sleep had done him the world of good. Up ahead of them was the famous golden arches sign of a McDonalds. 'Brilliant… I'm starving.' He said more to himself, rubbing the sleep from his face.

The driver parked up and opened his door as he stepped out into the afternoon sun. He stretched out his arms and inhaled heavily as the scent of the ferry port hit him. It was a combination of diesel fumes and sewage with a faint hint of sea salt. 'I'm getting a cuppa tea… you want one?' asked the driver as he scratched his backside absent minded as he looked around fighting a yawn.

'I hate tea, the sole reason for the downfall of the British Empire.' Replied the boy sternly, his eyes scanning the car park. 'Shall we say thirty minutes break before we continue our journey?'

'Suit yourself.' muttered the driver offishly.

The boy walked over to join the long queue at the services toilets as the driver wandered off into one of the overpriced shops again scratching his arse as he walked. Behind him stood three young boys that he could only assume were part of a European school trip; they spoke French with the noticeable tang of the Parisian districts. A somewhat 'street' Argot accent mostly heard in French Rap or a Pierre Morel movie. Having spent most of his earlier childhood in Europe following his father's work he had become fluent in both French and German. He chuckled at them, knowing from how well they spoke that these boys were most likely the heirs of wealthy businessmen and bankers. Their chosen inappropriate attire

and forced ghetto accents no more than a put-on performance as a form of rebellion and statement against their affluent parents. He listened and realised he was in luck as one of them bragged and boasted about their new mobile phones as the other two messed around by pushing him and begging him to stop and shut up.

'Qu'est-ce que vous voulez?' said one of the schoolboys as he turned to look at them. The young boy was dressed as though he belonged in a Rap music video, the side of his head was shaved into all sorts of intrinsic patterns and his left eyebrow had been shaved with three little lines, he assumed could only be to represent scars, however they looked like he had slipped with the clippers.

'Voulez-vous un nouveau téléphone?' he asked, showing them the one he had *borrowed* from Campbell earlier that morning.

'Que veux tu pour ça?' asked the cocky boy playing with his expensive gold chain around his neck.

'€350?' he said. 'Apple iPhone 11 Pro… Pas de mot de passe…' he said, shaking it provocatively in front of the younger schoolboys.

'Elle est cassée?' laughed the Parisian boy nervously now noticing the bruising around the English boy's face.

He laughed and put the phone in front of the Parisian's face and accessed some of the Apps and internet features. 'Pas cassé.' He replied with a half-smile.

'Il a fait beaucoup de blé…' smiled one of the other French boys as his friend handed over €350 in €50 notes. Typical affluent parents are always sending their young child abroad with excessive amounts of cash that they inevitably spend on crap that isn't relevant or associated with their trip.

'Tout le plaisir était pour moi.' Smiled the boy as he took the money. He decided to leave the three French boys before they changed their mind or had their mind changed for them by one of their accompanying teachers. He moved out of the queue to use the toilets in the restaurant instead. As he sat down, he checked his own personal phone, several missed calls from his Uncle Max. *'Not yet'* he said to himself as he locked his screen and went to order himself some lunch. He sat in silence as he ate. With each mouthful he realised how much he had missed the taste of the cheeseburgers, the salty fries and the crunchy nuggets. At Fettes College they were given high end meals prepared to restaurant quality dining, but like any child it was the simple greasy foods that he had longed for. He threw away his wrappers and made his way back outside to meet the driver who was already by the Mercedes V-Class MPV, dropping a cigarette to the tarmacked ground, squashing it into a smoking mulch under his foot.

He crossed the car park and noticed the French school bus parked up with the Parisian school children loitering noisily outside. The wannabe Rapper now showing off his new purchase to his envious peers, already playing loud obnoxious music from it. He diverted across to ensure he was spotted by the students as they loitered outside the bus. He spoke to the other students and managed to sell the second questionably obtained phone for more euros at a quarter of what they were worth, but he didn't care, and it was not as if Campbell and his idiot friends needed the money.

As he walked back to the Uber car, he reflected on how much fun the children outside of the bus were having, seeing the school kids messing about and interacting together. He felt a sensation of being cold inside, the feeling he had somehow inherited when he had first heard about his parent's demise in Chamonix three years before. The coldness manifested and grew throughout his torment over the past few years. For him, school was just years of isolation from interpersonal acts of harassment. Seeing how many new ways he would be subjected to intimidating hostile and degrading behaviour of his peers. He knew there were children undergoing much worse than him, those poor souls treated less fairly by

savage contemporaries. But for him the reality of the humiliating or offensive environment had toughened him, hardened him. He could see the cold expression in his own pale grey eyes when he looked into any mirror, the same serious look that his uncle or late father had displayed when the occasion called for it. His uncle's demeanour both the by-product and creation from his extensive experience, integral to his role in the Special Forces.

The journey south from Newcastle was uneventful and before he realised it, they pulled up along the banks of the Humber in Hull. He bid farewell to the Uber driver and took in his new surroundings.

Looking out over the Humber he recalled how his uncle had always told him stories of how Norfolk Fishermen further to the south took cash bribes to take criminals over to Belgium or Holland on their small fishing boats. That was before the *'pain-in-the-arse'* Clandestine Channel Threat Commander was initiated by the Home Office to tackle such illegal voyages. He watched as a high-powered Fast Response Targa 31 patrol boat roared past him, three border control officers stood in the rear of the vessel gripping their Heckler-Koch MP5 and G36 submachine guns as the dominant boat bounced along. He watched it disappear into the distant horizon as he stood a while in thought contemplating his next actions, weighing up all the risks. His mobile buzzed once more as he cancelled the call, the screen again showing his uncle's smiling face.

The bustling street of Holderness Road was filled with people shopping, tourists exploring, and university students sat in small groups enjoying the sunshine along the waterfront. Looking across he smiled to himself as he stood in admiration of a homeless man's talent busily busking for coins playing Salut d'Amour by Sir Edward Elgar on his violin. 'Perfect' he said to himself. The violin had always been special to him, his mother Monique had been an exceptional violinist. He'd sit and watch her play for hours when he was a small boy.

'Want to earn £250?' He called to the male on ending his piece as four bystanders applauded gently, a young child ran over and threw some coins into the open violin case before running off again.

'That must be one hell of a request… what you want me to play?' smiled the man in reply, shouldering his violin once more in preparation.

'I have a proposition for you…' he began, walking forward he whispered, 'How would you like to stay in a hotel for one night, have all your meals paid for and £250 in cash for your trouble?'

'What are you talking about kid?' replied the male curiously looking around them with caution.

'I need an adult to check-in at the hotel, I have no adult with me and I do not want to sleep rough with all my belongings.' He said shrugging his heavy bags on his shoulders. 'You of all people know the dangers of sleeping rough. You wouldn't want a little kid like me alone on the streets now, would you?'

'I'm not going into a bloody hotel room with you kid.' he retorted abruptly, 'Do you think I am mad?'

'Separate rooms naturally and cash up front.' The boy smiled in response, taking the cash out of his pocket waving it in front of the stranger. 'You will not see me or hear from me other than during the check-in process.'

'Where are your parents' kid?' asked the musician, again looking around.

'They're dead.' He replied coldly. 'You coming or not?' He spat as he gathered his belongings and set off for The Embassy Hotel on Hedon Road followed closely by the musician.

The hotel was of standard three-star accommodation, clean on the surface and pleasant enough throughout.

He deposited his belongings in the small room and thanked the musician. 'I need your discretion, not a word to anyone.' He said handing over the money as the musician nodded, pocketing the cash.

He walked out into the busy streets heading for the local cash point along the road. He took out the stolen cards and threw them into a bin outside the bank. He could not risk using them again to make any withdrawals. He needed to be invisible for as long as possible. He entered a questionable currency exchange shop and looked at the old north African male sitting indignantly behind the thick safety glass screen. The walls were covered in screens with current exchange rates and fees. The magnolia walls stained yellow from nicotine.

'Afternoon, I need to exchange sterling for euros.' He asked with a smile.

The north African looked unimpressed at the teenager and sniffed heavily as he opened the small hatch in the bottom of the safety glass. 'How much?' he hissed through missing teeth as he lit another cigarette from the butt of the one he'd just finished, the thick choking smoke issuing out from the small hole in the glass.

'£6500.' Replied the youth as he watched the shopkeepers' eyes widen in delight. 'And I want your best rate or I walk.'

Crossing the road to the train station he purchased a train ticket back to Kent to throw the police off his scent as they would be bound to check the bank records of his bank cards as soon as he had been reported missing by either the Head Dean of Fettes or his uncle Max.

The sun was still high in the sky above him, the benefit of a beautiful summer evening. After a short walk he arrived at the scuba store just as they were closing.

'What do you want?' asked a small stocky man from within the wet room hanging up sodden wet suits onto a large rack from a large barrel filled with water in front of him. The man was in his late forties and visibly very fit, his muscular physique apparent through his damp t-shirt and rolled down wetsuit.

'Good afternoon, I am here on behalf of Mr Albert Ross. We placed a large order earlier today. I'm here to collect.' Replied the boy confidently.

'Oh…' replied the man rubbing his hands on a pair of shorts hanging next to him as he walked around to meet him. 'I thought you would be a lot older… how old are you?' asked the man eyeing him closely as he scrutinised the young man in the grey hoodie standing in front of him.

'Is that relevant? My father has asked me to collect the items before it gets too late.' He replied nonchalantly checking his watch. 'If you'd rather he cancels the order we can go elsewhere?' He spat back indignantly, his arms now folded.

'No, no…' said the man holding up his hands to calm the situation. 'Follow me then. I'm Alex by the by. The owner.'

He followed the man around to the side of the building to a large lock up unit. The door was already open, and he could see it was full of diving gear, harnesses, weights and bottles of all colours, shapes and sizes.

'Welcome to Hull's finest dive supplier. You have ordered an interesting set, where are you intending to dive?' asked Alex inquisitively.

'Do you have everything we ordered?' he replied, ignoring the man's question.

'Yes, it's all here, although the bottles though have been a problem.' He said tapping the racking.

'What problem?' spat the boy indignantly, walking forward.

The man walked into the lock up and returned with two small bottles, one in each arm. 'The duration you need doesn't come in anything smaller than these six litres 230 bar. You'll need several of them.' He said putting them down in front of the young man. 'Unless you go really high-end. Besides… The duration you are looking at is far too long, that much gas in your system is dangerous. You'd be better off with a submersible.'

'These are far too large for what I… we need.' He said lifting one of the bottles, 'What is this three, four kilos?' he asked, estimating the weight of the tank. 'It will not be possible, not without sinking like a stone. I can't carry this many tanks without a trolley which is out of the question.'

'If you want to be down there for anything more than an hour at a time you need to upgrade the tank.' Replied the man, scratching at his stubbled cheek, 'For what you have requested, you will need a lot of these tanks… Or several twelve litre tanks.'

'There is no way I can carry all these.' He put a hand on his head, this was not what he had imagined. 'He knew too well the delicacy and importance of the weight / buoyancy ratio needed when diving. It had to be precise, or you'd sink to the bottom immediately.

'You will have to reduce the down time then.' Said Alex with a shrug.

'I was relying on you having what I asked for. And what you advertised.' He replied, shaking his head before looking back to the North Sea on the horizon.

'I can recommend a rebreather, that should, with a smaller cylinder and a special mix you can get three hours of dive time per bottle... But...'

'But what? That sounds perfect.' He questioned.

'Have you ever used a rebreather before? They can be very dangerous, if the gas mixture has too little oxygen...' said Alex seriously. 'Then there is the price... A rebreather is £3000, but we can hire it out for £600.'

Indignantly the young man handed over the additional money but after the larger bottles were removed it worked out as only £1370 with all the extra upgraded equipment. He kicked himself for throwing away all the *borrowed* bank cards, this additional cost had not been in his calculations but only set him back a little. He thoroughly checked the suit to ensure it could withstand many hours in water approximately 6 °C (43 °F) and that his weights were correct for what he needed. He took a taxi back to the hotel and with some discretion and furtive manoeuvres to avoid the staff he managed to get everything up to his room.

He locked the door and set about laying all the equipment on top of the bed, his clothes, folded tightly into his backpack which he then added into the waterproof dive bag he had just purchased along with the wet / dry suit and hood, buoyancy weights, fins, rebreather and tank and the three additional tanks laid out as he intended on wearing them. He stepped back to take it all in, he laughed to himself at the thought that filled his head. The equipment was arranged to look as though a diver had been laying on the bed before his body disappeared with only the clothing and equipment remaining. He collected the large box that he had brought with him from Mack the groundskeeper at Fettes earlier that day and opened it carefully. Meticulously he set about removing four large dark blue industrial size magnets used for magnet fishing. Each had been advertised as able to withstand or certainly take up to 300kg, but he knew that this was never actually the case, and this was why he ordered four of them. 'Better safer than sorry' he said to himself as he tied on individual lengths of 9.8mm climbing rope to each with climbing carabiners at the other end.

He took his phone from the table and sent a single text message. If he left it too long his uncle and aunt would call the police and his photograph would be everywhere. But if he sent it too soon, he knew his uncle would come looking.

<Dear Max and Charmian, I miss you both. I have begun a mammoth undertaking that required me to disappear. I am safe and well and needed some time to find myself. I will return home when I know who I am. I know you will, but please do not worry about me. I love you. James x>

He turned his phone off before removing the sim card from the back, using the hotel rooms complimentary glass ashtray as a beaker he took out his butane torch lighter, another of his Uncle Max's birthday gifts and swiftly melted the sim until it was a blob of molten plastic. He inserted a new sim, this one looked very different to any normal sim card, but he needed to be sure he would not be followed. His phone beeped into life, and he checked everything was working. Once satisfied he placed the phone into a heavy-duty holder that he had ordered some weeks before. It had been labelled as 'Indestructible' having a picture of an indignant incredible hulk trying to snap it in two and another of a 4x4 driving over it. Although it was shipped from China it was advertised as *combat ready*, stating that it was waterproof up to 300 metres, fire-proof and even able to withstand a bullet. As long as it did the first of these proficiently, he would be happy.

He cleared the bed and jumped in; his eyes were closed before his head sunk into the hotel beds soft pillow.

Chapter 3

The Crossing

The Humber, Hull.

His alarm went off at 22:30 PM. He yawned wide and stretched out his tired limbs, he had managed five hours but he had hardly slept soundly due to the excitement of what was to come. He rolled over and turned on the bedside table light before rubbing his tired eyes. He looked outside to see there had been a light shower since he went to bed, drips still ran down the old windowpane of the hotel room. He stared for a moment lost in thought at what lay ahead of him, the adventure, excitement and danger he somehow needed, and the new life he yearned for.

He dressed quickly into the diving suit and ate two bananas and downed a bottle of energy drink, he looked at himself in the mirror and took several deep breaths. 'This is it. Make a plan, stick to it.' he said aloud to his reflection.

Grabbing his backpack he slipped it on, then grabbed the two kit bags containing the remaining dive gear. Walking over to the door he turned to look at his other school belongings and the items he would not be needing. He had packaged them up and addressed them to his uncle and aunties home in Kent. He had left a message with the hotel reception that the items were to be collected by a private courier in the early hours, and that the courier was to be allowed into the room to collect the items.

He crept out of the dormant hotel and out of the rear of the building using a staff only door next to the empty kitchen. The streets of the surrounding industrial estate were deserted and silent other than the sound of incessant seagulls and the dozens of mast posts jangling and tapping in the cool breeze. He hurriedly made his way across the road by the roundabout and over the small embankment to the large maintenance mooring harbour of Alexandria Dock between the Siemens Gamesa Renewable Energy depot and training centre on the other side of the harbour.

Checking all was quiet he walked down to the access path to the side of one of the large cargo ships anchored there. Using the dozens of wind turbine fin propellers lying in prostration across the yard as cover as he crept to the edge of the harbour lock gate. The night was cool but not cold and the walk carrying the heavy equipment had warmed him up to a light sweat, not helped by the thick restricting dry suit that he had already put on when back in the hotel.

Walking into a jog he crossed the gate over to the Siemens Gamesa Training Centre before making his way down to the muddy banks of the Humber. The old rotting wooden posts emerged from the still dark water like gnarled giant green fingers. He sat with his legs in the water, unzipping the first holdall removing the webbing and harness. Slipping it on and fastening it at the front, adding the diving weights made his shoulders droop slightly. He slid on his waterproof backpack over the top again clipping the chest and waist supports before taking out the first of the bottles from the second holdall. He fastened them onto his webbing so that they hung from the back. The large fishing magnets were then clipped to the front of the webbing. He connected the rebreather to the fourth bottle and tapped the dials gently. A distant noise made him freeze on the stop, he held his breath and leant down low against the damp hard wood of the jetty. His pale eyes scanned the horizon but only a disturbed seagull flapped indignantly atop one of the far-off posts above the dark water. Rolling the two holdalls up he slipped them into the side pockets of his backpack for use later on. The fins were the last item to go on as he lowered himself fully into the chilly still water, even with the equipment and dry suit he could feel the icy touch of the North Sea against his skin. He lowered the full-face mask and checked the rebreather once more, taking three breaths to check the dials and mixture level. Checking the time on his Omega Seamaster wristwatch he looked to the east to see the large ferry's stern moored at the terminal 600 metres away. He closed his eyes before silently disappearing beneath the black water, leaving no trace that he had been there at all.

He swam slow and steady against the current until he was alongside the training centre, he pushed on to the Hull Ferry Terminal pier where he could make out the five large support pylons that acted as barriers to the cargo load of the ferry. The sky was dark and moonless and the water as black as an abyss, but he remained at a depth of two metres to ensure he was not seen before coming up on the starboard side of the behemoth ferry. He had studied this particular ferry and recalled its impressive length of 212 m / 696 ft from bow to stern. He had decided to travel closer to the bow just in case the magnets failed him as he wanted more time to swim away before he would be inevitably sucked into the vast propellor blades and rudder at the rear. He could hear the loud engines from within the large ferry roar into life as he tread the calm water by its side, the rear of the vessel frothed and splashed as the large propellor ripped the still water beneath. Checking his watch, he could see that it was already 23:20 PM, he only had ten minutes before it would leave for Rotterdam. He quickly unclipped one of the fishing magnets from his harness and attached it to the hull just above water level, ensuring it fixed fast he gripped it hard in his right hand and rested his legs letting the large magnet take his full body weight. Once he was happy it would hold, he unclipped another magnet and secured it higher up on the ship's blue hull this time above the draft line. He heard a familiar sound of a smaller boat behind him as he shot around to see the high-powered Fast Response Targa 31 patrol boat speeding towards him, spotlight on and scanning the water as it thundered along. He swore to himself as he released the climbing rope in his right hand causing him to sink beneath the wave silently, his dark suit and equipment instantly disappearing into the Humber. He could make out the bright spotlight above through the murky and muddy water as it scanned the hull as it passed. He had intentionally chosen dark blue magnets for this very reason. The patrol boat continued past without stopping, the young female border control officer not able to distinguish the two dark blue circles against the large, dark blue panelled hull of the mighty vessel. He waited for the Targa to disappear before he hurriedly swam back to the surface.

He could hear the rear opening stern hiss closed after all the passengers and cargo had been boarded, he squinted as the powerful engines raised to a deafening crescendo of a roar as he was pulled forward like a puppet lifted by its string with the sudden propulsion movement of the giant vessel. He hastily clipped the last two magnets onto the vessel as a safety precaution, firstly he did not want to come detached halfway across the North Sea, and secondly, he did not want to end up anywhere near the deadly propellor at the rear of the ship 150 metres off to his left. He once again sank below the water letting the slack in the rope tighten as he was dragged through the freezing water. He laughed through the mouthpiece of the rebreather as he recalled the sensation of skydiving, his body filled with that unnatural buzz that he had felt when he had first jumped from a small aircraft some years earlier. A typically bizarre birthday present from his uncle Max. *"Experiences are what life is all about."* He would say to him.

The ferry made fast progress along the Humber and they were soon clear of Grimsby behind him to his right and the arm of the Spurn on the opposite bank to the left as they entered the vast North Sea. He knew the vessel would soon be at full speed of 22 knots / 25 mph which would test the durability of the magnets that he now had to entrust with his life, but also the physical and mental stability and endurance of his own body. He was fit and healthy, as any other fourteen-year-old was. But he had excelled in the water and had even turned down an invitation when he had been approached by the under 18's British Olympic swimming team. Years of making use of the dozens of hotel swimming pools when travelling with his parents as a younger child now put to good use. The icy water ripped suddenly at the back of his neck, as he raised his hands to see what had happened, he felt a loose Velcro tag flapping behind his head, it had somehow come unattached from the thick suit and hood that covered every part of his body. He tightened the Velcro to stem the cold water which made it a little more bearable as he once again checked his watch, 'Eleven hours to go' he said to himself as he was laid flat fully submerged being towed alongside the massive P&O Ferry across the North Sea.

After an hour had passed, he pulled himself up to above the surface, he was shocked at how hard this was against the strong force of the water. He looked first to the magnets and breathed a sigh of relief that all four were all still intact and doing their job tightly fixed to the large hull. He then looked behind him to the distant lights that were now specks on the black horizon, 'Goodbye England...' he said to himself. Looking forward he could only see darkness. The sky was a sombre shade of black and the sea similar to obsidian. He tied off one of the climbing ropes to save his right hand from cramping so that he could hang free above the water, resting his mouth by removing the rebreather and full-face mask. The crispness of the cold air and spray from the giant bow wake ahead of him was invigorating to say the least. He smiled, for the first time in nearly three years he actually felt alive. He rested his eyes from the spray as he bobbed up and down from the rock of the lapping waves beneath him, the gentle and soothing motion extremely relaxing on his tired and cold body. His eyes felt heavy, and all went quiet.

He woke suddenly with a start as his shoulders fell into the freezing waters. His face splashed by the sudden loss of tension as he pulled on the face mask and rebreather in a shock of panic. 'What the…?' he squealed as he looked above him to see one of the magnets had fallen off, the one he had tied himself up to. The three remaining magnets still held fast as he caught his breath and took in what was going on. The fallen magnet now acted as a small disc shaped anchor, pulling him down as he scrambled and felt around for the right rope. He gripped the end that was attached to the carabiner on his chest harness and pulled it up as quickly as he could with both hands. His cold and tired arms struggled against the dragging weight as it was pulled back up through the water. With a sigh he reattached the magnet to the hull and gave it a test pull only to find it came off straight away in his hand. He looked at the other side to see the magnet had fallen out of the outer casing completely, now lost somewhere at the bottom of the North Sea.

He set about untying the heavy magnet casing and dropped it into the vast sea as fast as he could, not wanting the extra weight dragging behind him again, in case one or all the remaining magnets decided to follow suit.

Deciding to keep his face mask on, for warmth more than anything, he tied all three ropes off to spread the weight, wanting to avoid another failure. He lay back once more now half out of the water so that he had only his legs submerged in the water. The suction from the ship's wake making his legs and long finned feet pull down towards the darkness beneath the deep keel below. As the hours passed, he changed the bottle of mixture within the rebreather and again with the monotonous rhythmic motion from the waves he again fell asleep. The adrenaline was still pumping through him uncontrollably, but his body was now fatigued and at the point of exhaustion.

He woke to a blue sky above him, clear of clouds and the spectacular sight of the sun rising before him to the east. Shaking the face mask off he again happily breathed in the fresh air filling his lungs. He checked the dial to see he had only 15 minutes of mixture left, annoyed with himself that the alarm had not warned him of this he again changed to the third bottle. His watch read 05:12 AM, and he knew the ferry would be landing at Rotterdam port at 10:00 AM. An indignant rumble from his stomach made him look down, he had not eaten anything in nearly seven hours, and that had only been two bananas.

He pulled the waterproof bag from his back and removed another banana which he ate greedily, he threw the skin over his shoulder not thinking anything of it, it was biodegradable but then he thought 'What if someone saw it?'. He looked up to the gunwale fifty feet above him to see if anyone was there but then shook his head in frustration, 'Moron, you're being stupid… who is going to see that.' The exposure to the cold was taking its toll on him mentally.

Finishing his small meal and several cereal protein bars, he closed the bag and pulled it back onto his shoulders when he heard a splash from behind him. To his left he saw one of the bottles of air mixture bob away to the rear of the vessel. He grabbed at his back as he realised he had displaced his last tank when putting his backpack on. 'No!' he bit his lip. Twisting around he checked the dials of the remaining two he had clipped onto his belt only to confirm that they were indeed the two empty bottles, and it was in fact the last full bottle now being sucked into the propeller at the rear of the ferry. 'That changes things then…' he said to himself as he turned off the oxygen and mixture tank.

He racked his exhausted brain and checked his watch again. He only has 2-3 hours of air left and just over four hours of the voyage left. He would now need to stay above the water for the duration of the voyage in plain sight of any passing boats thanks to the beautiful morning sunlight. 'At 08:00 AM I can go back down, but that leaves two whole hours of sitting in full sight of whomever passes… literally as sitting duck…' he said aloud to himself as though to reassure his own mind before it started to panic.

The first hour felt like it dragged on, he checked his watch every five minutes, and the monotonous scenery of the great expanse of the North Sea did not help the time passing. As it slowly approached 07:45 AM he prepared himself to return beneath the waves. Untying the knot of the climbing rope attached to the three remaining magnets he slipped back into the water, lowering himself down with his arms. One metre below, two metres below then the slack tightened and again it was like he was skydiving but under water. He regulated his breathing ensuring he managed the mixture as best he could, regularly checking the dials and his watch to confirm all were in order.

09:00 AM came and went and he pulled himself up so that his face was breaking the surface water. On the horizon he could see a long thin and very flat dark smudge along the skyline, Holland.

Between the ferry and the landmass were hundreds of vessels, some huge cargo tankers, some small ferries like the one he was hitchhiking with, and others were small private vessels going about their business. The water here had a much stronger current that knocked him against the side of the hull. He decided to see if the effect would lessen by being beneath the water, so he slipped back under the waves using the tension of the rope to tighten and hold him steady. As he reached the two-metre depth, he felt himself go a little deeper. Looking around to see if this was just the current, he tried to steady himself. He noticed the ferry had slowed to approximately 15 knots / 15 mph for the last leg of the approach to its destination. He checked the depth gauge on his harness, and it read three metres, then three and a half metres... Four metres and it was getting slightly darker. Something was going wrong.

He swam back up to the surface to see the three magnets had all moved down below the water draft line. As he pulled on them to climb up out of the water, they continued to drag along the hull lowering with each movement. The more he desperately pulled the more they sank closer to the waves now just below. Now frantic he launched himself up to grab one of the magnets. The blue casing came off in his hand and the magnet stayed attached to the vast hull. 'Oh no!!' he thought.

With only two magnets holding him to the side of the vessel he was losing traction fast. As before he untied the rope to ease the extra weight of the heavy magnet housing, he tied a bowline knot around the magnet and pulled down with all his weight as the rope tightened, it had worked. But now he had to kick furiously to keep himself up above the water as the magnets kept sinking below the water line. Their purpose now obsolete; he had to find another way to stay buoyant until he was closer to shore.

His tired eyes shot desperately around the hull to see if there was any where he could tie himself to, a hand hold or cleat, anything he could use. Anxiously he tried to grip the smooth surface of the hull with his wetsuit gloves but obviously to no avail as he slid beneath the waves.

The dark smudge of the horizon grew clearer as Holland came quickly into focus. The endless flat landscape formed a crescent around the horizon as the sunlight cleared the distant haze. He assumed he was only ten miles away from the shore and harbour of the Europoort Rotterdam and checking his watch this was confirmed, 0927 AM. He could now make out the series of cranes off to his right that banked the harbour and cargo depots. To his left and running the length of the shore he saw the pale sand stretch off for what must have been sixty kilometres, all utterly flat and featureless. He cupped his hands around the caseless magnet for stability as the remaining magnets stabilised. '30 minutes is all I need' he spat to himself through the face mask as he reattached the rebreather and checked his dial, '23% left.' he said aloud, 'It will have to do.'

His eyes scanned the waters around him as dozens of behemoth cargo transporters filled the dark green waters. Their massive hulls low from the hundreds of cargo containers stacked neatly above. To the right he saw the majority of the vessels carefully manoeuvre into the Hutchison Ports ECT Euromax terminal. This is where things got really difficult. For the past three months he had planned every step of the journey and every eventuality or potential hazard. His evenings had been spent in the College library using his phone and laptop to research his route from Edinburgh down to Hull, then his clandestine crossing into Rotterdam. He had read that this port was one of the busiest in Europe and he knew full well that the traffic here would be treacherous, but on seeing the dozens of monstrous vessels between him and his target was truly breathtaking. No amount of computer research could prepare anyone for what lay before him. He lowered himself below the water as more ships came closer, he could not allow himself to be discovered, no now after everything he had done. Dropping back to two metres depth he eyed his Omega watch closely, its beautiful blue dial reflecting the sun above him as the seconds hand rotated effortlessly around on its continuous movement. The movement of the watch had been the reason his father had always worn an Omega. And was the reason why his father had purchased this very watch for him on his eleventh birthday, it was made more sentimental as it happened to be purchased and gifted just the month before their unexpected demise that December.

The ferry bellowed out a longhorn to ensure the other vessels knew it was there, curious considering it was gigantic in itself and not at all inconspicuous.

The ferry slowed to a crawling pace of 5 knots / 5 MPH as it made for its last approach into the harbour and the Nieuwe waterweg. 'This is it' he swallowed as he readied himself. He disconnected the solitary magnets bowline knot and one of the working magnets from the hull and let them drop into the deep sea. He hated the idea of polluting the waters, but he just could not carry the weight at this time. With only one magnet attached he slipped deeper beneath the water, he readied himself for the last and undoubtedly the most treacherous stretch of his perilous journey.

He had dived in many countries with his family and was more than comfortable under the water, but the mental image of being sucked into the huge propeller kept flooding his mind. Clearing his mind of all negative thoughts he ran through his objective one last time. Pushing off from the starboard side he would need to swim hard and fast to ensure he was not sucked backwards and under the hull by the wake and into the blades of the propeller at the rear of the ferry. Raising his legs behind him, he used the now solitary rope over his shoulder to stabilise himself as he unclipped the last magnet. Instantly he began to be pushed along by the force of the muddy water so without hesitation he took his chance. He kicked off with all of his remaining strength, downwards to begin with before levelling off to a horizontal position. His large fins made his progress greater than he could have hoped. He swam for a solid thirty seconds before he allowed himself to look behind him. The ferry had continued into the Nieuwe waterweg shipping canal as he was left alone beneath the waves in the centre of the slip of the huge storm surge barrier that ran along the canal was still no safe place to be, with all the container ships and other vessels making their way in and out he had to move fast. The ferry was now well clear, and he had to act fast. Grabbing the dive compass on his webbing harness he checked his bearing in the murky and densely muddied water. Kicking with everything he had left he made his way back across the 600 metres of open sea to the man-made sea defence structure, De Pier Hoek van Holland that jutted out of the featureless landscape. His tired legs motored on as the alarm on his dial told him he only had 10% of mixture left in his tank, he moved closer to the surface to better see the dial. His head was only a metre below the surface when he heard a deafening bellow from somewhere behind him.

His head shot around just in time to see another large vessel motoring towards him, its immense white bow only metres behind him ripping a large wake in the otherwise calm sea. He continued away from it, but the ship was just too large as it overwhelmed him entirely. He was forced against the solid bow with a heavy thud that winded him causing him to breath in quick and shallow breaths, each one agony. His arms knocked against the bow as he rolled helplessly underneath, his legs still kicking furiously to the side to get clear. His body continued to roll uncontrollably underneath the vessel as he attempted to steady himself. The tank on his back knocked him all over the place with each attempt. He could hear the engine from within as his head banged off the keel knocking his face mask askew letting in a torrent of the freezing murky water making him force his eyes closed.

His senses failed him completely as he could no longer see, the engine from within the belly of the large ship roared above him and his balance had been shocked by the violent rolling beneath the ship's massive flat keel. He suddenly found himself dismayed and feeling very scared. 'What am I doing!' he shouted to himself as his mind struggled to think. His mind filled with hundreds of ideas but none that would actually help him out of his ordeal, until he recalled a survival programme he had seen some years ago about what to do should you find yourself in the middle of an avalanche. 'Really brain... this is all you can come up with...' he spat indignantly as he continued to roll underneath the huge keel towards the thrashing propellers. But then he realised what his brain was telling him to do. He suddenly moved his arms up to cover his head to save it from being thrown aggressively against the barnacle infested keel. Then he moved his arms out, stretching them to make a star shape. His legs copied the movement instantaneously. This surprisingly stopped him from spinning almost suddenly. Now stationary, he found himself laying static belly up facing the bottom of the vessel, 'Now I know which way is up...'. With a swift movement he placed his right hand on the top of the mask and jutted his jaw out. Pushing down on the ridge of his eyebrows he inhaled a deep breath before exhaling out through his nose forcing out the oxygen in his lungs as he pulled the mask away from his forehead ever so slightly, this simultaneously removed all the water from inside his face mask but also allowed him to see his surroundings. The alarm beeped once more, without looking he knew he only had 5% mixture left. His eyes shot to his side as he saw the swirling rotating blades of the vessel's propeller not ten metres away.

Spitting out the rebreather he screamed, 'Jesus!!!' He shouted in despair releasing millions of tiny air bubbles, his eyes wide taking in the terror swiftly approaching him. Pulling up his legs to behind his buttocks he pushed off the bottom of the vessel as hard as he could, his exhausted legs kicking him downwards as he used his hands and tongue to move the rebreather back into his mouth. He bit down on the mouthpiece as his burning legs roared in protest. The alarm on the dial once again beeped to advise he had now gone past the safety level of 5% mixture in the tank. The vessel continued forward above him but the powerful propeller sucked him upward towards the surface and the spinning blades. He screamed into the mouthpiece as he began to swim with both legs together as though performing the butterfly stroke or as a mermaid would use their tailfin. He kicked and kicked until suddenly the pulling from above passed and he dropped with some force from the momentum of his last few kicks. He continued to scream as he levelled off again, his body ached everywhere, his lungs were tight and screaming at him to stop, and his body, now beyond exhausted from the swimming, was numb and shaking with fatigue. He closed his eyes as the vacant adrenaline evaporated any energy he had left and the prolonged exposure to the cold water took over. His body started shutting down. He dreamt of sleep, but he was tenacious and somehow, he fought on. Once again, he checked the compass and readied himself before making for the pier and Terra Firma.

The man made pier was constructed as a sea defence from coastal erosion, the rough North Sea and relentless shipping had caused so much damage to the coast that this was the obvious solution. The sides were made up of huge cuboids of solid rock piled haphazardly upon another and in between these two man made shorelines ran a fifteen-foot-wide path that stretched nearly a kilometre out to sea.

He climbed the dark cuboids and took off the large diving fins clipping them to his harness so that they hung around his waist. Looking over he could see two elderly men sat further down the pier looking off into the distance past the large red pylon at the far end. The beacon that marked the end of De Pier Hoek van Holland. He dragged himself up the coarse abrasive blocks until he lay next to the path. Checking that there was nobody in sight he made his way across to the other side of the pier and onto the blocks on the other side. He performed a swan dive off the top of them into the water below on the other side, the water here much clearer, his mask enabling him to see the pale sand below him. He let the current take his mangled and fatigued body along and closer to the sandy shore past the Hook of Holland so that he was in a more remote spot, free of ramblers and sightseers.

Kicking loosely, limply and sporadically his body rose and fell with the small waves ebb until he had reached the centre of the long sandy beach. His feet now touching the seabed he walked towards the shallows. He lay in the shallow water on his back as he ripped off the mask and mouthpiece he took in the fresh oxygen and laughed as tears fell down his quivering cheeks.

He had made it.

Chapter 4

The New Life

Hook of Holland / Monster, Rotterdam.

Along the beach in the far distance, he could see several dog walkers and a solitary kite surfer. Other than these few members of the public he was alone and had the beach to himself. He took off his backpack, the harness and tanks and threw everything onto the sand before he took off the wet / dry suit. Laying in his shorts and t-shirt he allowed the refreshing water to cover him entirely for five minutes. Not having access to a toilet during the crossing he had no other option than to urinate inside the wet suit. The cool sea water also felt soothing against his bruised and burning muscles.

A broad smile covered his face as he looked up at the sun above him. He shook his head at the thought of what he had just accomplished. Eleven hours ago, he was standing on the banks of the Humber in Hull, England, now he had successfully made his way into Europe. And not one single person in the world knew about it. His tired hands played in the sand as the waves washed over him. He felt like sleeping right there and then. But he knew that if he was seen, or worse questioned or caught by the authorities he would be in serious trouble. No country's government took illegal entry lightly, not even as a minor.

Unpacking his backpack, he removed one of the large, folded kit holdall bags that he had used to carry the equipment down from the hotel the previous evening. He changed into some dry clothing before he rolled up the wetsuit and fins and placed them neatly inside the large bag before he zipped it up. The bag was far more spacious and lighter without the magnets or additional air tank. His intention was that should anyone now pass he would look nothing more than a young boy who had been for a morning swim on the beautiful summer morning.

He climbed the small ridge where the sand gave way to rough green grassy vegetation. Over the top he could make out the small villages that had over time become one large mass of residential and commercial buildings along with the large ugly grey industrial estates that always accompanied the sea ports. Making his way along the beach he could see the busier streets where families were walking, couples talking, people cycling and some eating late breakfasts or early lunches outside their apartments. At the smell and sight of the latter he checked his watch, 11:27 AM and his stomach once again roared into a growl of protest as he felt hunger strike hard within his tired body.

From the research he had completed before he left, he knew of several beach restaurants that were only a few hundred metres away that would provide him with the sustenance that he desired. Walking along the beach he inhaled the fresh salty air, amazed at how different and clean it smelt from the air back in England. Reaching his destination of a nearest beach restaurant he sat down in a small sofa chair and threw his bags at his feet and relaxed, sinking into the comfortable chair as his fatigue took hold. A young walnut haired waitress smiled as she approached him speaking in Dutch, she looked at his blank face then repeated in English,

'Good morning sir, what can I get for you?' her beautiful accent heavy with the Dutch 'ch' at the end of some of the words.

He looked at one of the menus on the glass topped table and scanned it quickly as she stared at him, pen and paper in hand. Ready to take his order. His brain was scrambled by his tiredness, he rubbed his eyes and looked at her with a smile, 'What would you recommend?'

'Wentelteefjes, Boterham or Uitsmijter are all good here.' She smiled confidently.

'I will have one of each and a large black coffee please.' He smiled again as she laughed playfully at him.

'What is your name?' she asked inquisitively, putting down her pad. Her eyes moved up and down taking him all in.

'Bond...' he replied. 'James Bond.'

'Welcome to Holland, Mr Bond.' The waitress nodded and scribbled his name on the order slip and walked back to the bar. It later transpired that the foods he had unknowingly ordered were, Wentelteefjes - sliced bread dipped in a mixture of egg and milk before being pan fried and topped with sweet jam. The Boterham transpired to be a grilled cheese and ham sandwich and Uitsmijter was a thin bacon or ham and egg on toast topped with cheese. The waitress had carried the three plates over to his table with a giggle but was amazed at how he managed to eat it all before he sat back to watch the beach goers.

As the morning progressed more people started arriving at the beach from the many camping sites and hotels in the area just back from the beach. His goal was one of the smaller hostels where they were unlikely to check his passport or challenge his appearance when he would have to lie to their faces telling them he was 16 years old. He looked older than he was and there was no doubt he had a certain maturity for his age, but no accommodation would let a 14-year-old check in or stay without calling the authorities first, he just hoped that he would persuade the staff so that he could get some well needed sleep.

He opened his tired eyes and looked up to see the young waitress standing beside him with the bill. She was no more than 16 years old and had a slim athletic build, her shoulders broad – those of a professional swimmer, her walnut hair was long and curly and her eyes a gentle auburn with a green fleck. She wore a loose flowery skirt hemmed just above her knee and white logoed t-shirt underneath a long apron that bore the restaurant's brand.

'What has brought you to Holland Mr Bond?' she asked, watching his eyes as he took out some money from his pocket.

'I am looking for something… and someone, a family friend.' He replied vaguely, handing her a €50 note, 'Keep the change.'

'Have you just come off the ferry?' she asked, looking at his bags beneath the table.

'Well, aren't you observant…' he smiled, 'Technically… in a sense, yes.'

She frowned at him and looked around, 'Did you travel alone? Where are your parents?'

James coughed and looked away before smiling again, 'They passed away. I am all alone.'

'I'm so sorry.' She replied holding her hand over her mouth, the other moving in to hold his on the glass top table. 'Is this why you're looking for the family friend?' she continued. 'My name is Lotte. Lotte de Kok.'

'Well of course you are…' he replied subtly, his gentle smile turning into a broader grin.

'Here take my number.' She scribbled down her phone number on the top of the bill. 'My father owns this restaurant. If you need any help… Please ask.' she nodded and smiled deeply.

'This is extremely generous of you Lotte, thank you very much.' James replied with a sincere smile, his hand still under hers on the table. 'Could you recommend somewhere to stay?'

The young waitress smiled and looked over to the man behind the bar before she turned back to James, 'We rent several huts along the seafront, on the Dunes down there.' She bit her lip then said, 'Hold on, yes?' as she ran over to the bar to speak to the man standing there. After two minutes he nodded and handed her a key. Running back over to James she placed the key next to his hand. 'They are basic but affordable, €45 a night should you like one?'

James took the key and looked her in the eye, 'Thank you.' He did not have the energy to tell her that her charity was not 100% true. He did not know how to tell her that his parents had actually passed some three years before. But he knew when to accept a blessing, so he kept his mouth shut and pocketed the key.

'James…' she started. 'I finish at 20:00 PM if you want to have a beer with me?' she said coyly. 'I don't suppose you know anyone here. You could be my guest?'

'That would be lovely Lotte. Again… Thank you so much.' He smiled at her and shouldered his backpack and picked up the large kit bag before making his way back onto the beach for the hut he would call home for the night. As he walked along the sandy beach, he realised that he had never actually been on a proper date or drunk beer before and had no idea what he was going to do, but for now he needed sleep… and a shower – he laughed sniffing his underarm. 'Still got a date smelling like a vagrant's big toe.' His mind raced back to the comments from his school friends but somehow they didn't have any effect on him anymore.

The hut was humble but comfortable with a soft bed, two-seater sofa, small dining table, wood burner and a small kitchenette, at the rear was a small toilet and shower cubicle. It resembled a static caravan that had been squashed and elongated at the ends. He stripped down and leant against the plastic wall of the shower as the hot water bore down on him. After ten minutes he threw on a towel and emptied the wet suit and equipment into the shower to wash it down. He used one of the hangers from the cupboard to hang it up in the shower cubicle before he climbed into the bed as the world around him fell into sudden darkness.

He woke with a start as an alarm filled his head, taking a minute to realise where he was. On seeing the North Sea outside he relaxed. He turned off his phone alarm and sat up scratching his still tired head. 19:30 PM he had only slept for just over six hours. He dressed in Chinos and a casual blue shirt but opted for sandals as the evening was still warm.

He walked up to the restaurant to see Lotte talking to the man at the bar. He approached and greeted them both.

'Good evening, I wanted to thank you for the hut… Would I be able to rent it for a few more nights? I can pay in full now of course.' He said handing over several €50 notes. Which the man took and nodded kindly in reply.

'Bier?' asked the man in return.

At which James looked at Lotte, she could see he was a little lost but grinned at him taking his arm sincerely. 'In Holland you can drink beer and wine at 16 years old, but you need to be 18 years old to purchase spirits.' Smiled Lotte.

James relaxed as she held his arm, her warm hand felt so nice against his skin. He had not been held affectionately like this since leaving his Aunty back in England. Affection was seldom seen or given in boarding schools. He looked at the large glass beer tankards sitting behind the bar and smiled, but became serious as he spoke, 'I'm honestly not much of a drinker… Would it be okay if I stuck to soft drinks?'

'You're sweet, most English cannot wait to drink when they come here.' She laughed, taking their drinks from the bar. 'Come on.' She took his hand and led him down to the beach.

'Was that your father?' asked James pointing back over his shoulder to the restaurant behind them.

'Ja, he is the owner.' She drank her beer and licked her lips. James paused for a moment and took in her flawless features. Her soft skin, her kind eyes, high cheekbones and her delicate plump lips.

'It is a beautiful location, have you worked here for a long time?' James asked as he looked around them, the beach was filled with people enjoying the summer evening. He turned back to her and in doing so knocked over his soft drink, he watched as the dark liquid sizzled into the sand leaving only frothy bubbles. 'Smooth' he said to himself, extremely embarrassed.

'My father likes to keep me close, and this is ideal. I have worked here for the past two summers, but my father has owned the restaurant for many years.' She took a long sip from her beer and looked at James intently. 'I want to talk about you…' she said, moving in closer to him. 'Tell me about yourself James.'

'I don't normally talk about myself really. Never had anyone ask me other than my uncle and aunt… but they know me better than anyone to be honest. They have looked after me since my parents…' he paused and looked down to the sand beneath them. Lotte passed him her beer and gestured for him to try some, which he did.

'Is that who you are looking for here? Your Uncle and Aunt?' she asked quietly.

'They are in England.' He replied looking out back to England across the sea. 'And probably worried sick,' he said more to himself. 'No, Lotte. I came here to find something... to find myself, the real me. And to find my uncle's friend.' He said taking another swig of beer, the taste becoming more and more agreeable. 'My uncle Max has an old friend called Jared Bruce. He is ex special forces and works in security at a club in Amsterdam.' He started, before he laughed aloud.

'What is it?' asked Lotte, taken aback by his laugh. 'Is it me?' He could see she felt hurt.

'Heavens no Lotte... I just recalled what my uncle once told me about him, Jared I mean. Jared is known as the Sac Spider, one of the world's deadliest spiders... a moniker from his army days, he has a spider tattoo on his neck and everything... but my uncle Max told me it is due to him being born with three testicles.' At this they both started laughing. They took it in turns drinking from the large bottle of beer as they continued their conversation.

'My uncle is an interesting man, he used to tell me stories of how he and Jared used to run covert missions in and out of Biggin Hill for the British Home Office.' He saw her confused eyes so reiterated for her, 'Biggin Hill is an old airfield outside of London. It was used during the second world war to counter the Luftwaffe bombers sent over from Germany and France. Supposedly disused by the military but it is actually the go-to location for world governments and secret service drop offs. My uncle and Jared specialised in black ops, the 'need to know' jobs that left them with heads full of dangerous knowledge and specific intelligence that was later believed by some to be a threat to British security.' Lotte held his arm again and leant in.

'I wanted to know about you James, not your uncle or his friends... Where were you born?' Lotte asked inquisitively.

'Glen Coe, Scotland.' He replied.

'You don't sound Scottish though.' She laughed.

'That is because we, my parents and I travelled around a lot. My mother was from Canton de Vaud, Switzerland and my father worked in selling armaments throughout Europe.' He swigged again, 'My parents also sent me to boarding schools where you soon learn accents are not assets. It is better to fit in, camouflage yourself to disappear within the surroundings.'

'That sounds horrible James…' Lotte retorted. 'Is that what happened to your face?' she said, stroking his bruised cheek and nose.

'This was a leaving present from my peers.' He frowned, 'You should have seen the other guy.' He laughed. 'Another drink?' he said, jumping up to his feet as his head rolled inside. 'Wow…' his eyes spun in his head as the ground wobbled beneath his feet.

'You okay James?' asked Lotte standing up next to him.

'Yes, I'm fine… I bumped my head earlier on under the… When on the ferry. Still a little dizzy.' He said as his mind's-eye flashed back to the underside of the large vessel earlier that morning where his head had smacked the keel several times.

'That would be the bier…' laughed Lotte, 'Here in Holland we drink the good stuff, too strong for British tummies.' They shared a laugh as he helped her up from the sand. Their faces were close enough to feel each other's breath.

'Dinner Lotte? I am ravenous…' smiled James, 'My treat, anywhere you like.'

'I know the best place in town.' Replied Lotte with a wry smile.

'Is it far?' asked James, brushing the sand from his trousers.

'Oh, it is not far… It is right over… there.' She said gesturing back up to her father's restaurant.

The restaurant was now a hive of activity with nearly every table occupied. Lotte's father had moved back into the kitchen and was now accompanied by three other people behind the bar and four waiters had taken over running the services around to the customers. Lotte and James chose a table nearest the beach and furthest away from her father's sharp eye. James had noticed how the staff also kept an eye on him every time they passed their table.

'Lotte, I feel a little awkward here. Somehow exposed…' James started looking around.

'Relax… They are all my relatives. We are all family.' She replied calmly. 'You're safe.'

Lotte ordered for them both as James tried his hardest to look calm with every passing of the observant staff. The food was exceptional and his company sensational. Lotte was right about her father being the best cook in town. The couple talked for several hours before they enjoyed a walk along the beach as the sun set off to the west. James carried her shoes, and he held his flip flops as they paddled through the shallow waters. It was a new moon and inexplicably dark above, a blanket of shimmering stars shone and twinkled brightly as the waves ebbed and flowed soothingly beneath their feet. They held hands as they walked until Lotte stopped abruptly pulling him back to her, their eyes locked as James held her close as they embraced tightly, their lips touched slowly as they kissed one another beneath the starry night sky.

'Good night, Mr Bond.' She whispered before she took her shoes and walked away back along the beach. She turned after a few steps and waved at him before running back towards the restaurant.

James woke to the sound of seagulls complaining and squawking loudly outside his hut. His mouth was bone dry and his head throbbed from the strong beer that he had consumed the previous night. He stretched the sleep from his limbs and opened his emails on his phone to find seven new messages from his uncle Max. The special chip he had inserted into his phone converted text messages into emails.

Message 1 14:34:03 <James, you must call me. I have just spoken to Fettes. What is going on? Max>

Message 2 14:56:34 <James, call me now please.>

Message 3 15:20:51 <James, what are you playing at?>

Message 4 15:35:16 <This is no game young man, call me now please.>

Message 5 16:00:03 <Fine, we will play it your way… I warned you.>

Message 6 16:37:20 <Uber trip from Edinburgh to Hull, train ticket from Hull to Kent, but you never boarded the train… Why has your phone been disabled? I trust you are no longer at the Embassy Hotel. What game are you playing boy?>

James knew his uncle still had contacts in the government and various police forces, contacts that he had clearly asked to run checks on him, and from the text message timings it only took him 37 minutes to glean all the intelligence on his bank account and get a location on his mobile phones IMEI and GPS via a Police Cell Site trace. His uncle had been the one who advised him about Ghost Chip Sim Cards and how to go 'off-line' making it impossible for any party to conduct unwanted data searches or location tracking. He'd taken this into account back at the Embassy Hotel before his crossing.

Message 7 16:52:45 <James… Must I begin the hunt?>

James smiled at this message. Ever since he was a small boy his uncle had played games with him. Taught him about escape and evasion, or

'Spec-ops hide and seek' as his uncle used to call it. They used to take it in turns to *hunt* each other around his family home and grounds of Skyfall in Glen Coe. His uncle Max always used to start by counting to 60 seconds before shouting 'Let's begin the hunt!'

Reply: <Uncle Max, I am safe and well. Please do not worry. I knew you would not allow me to leave hence my actions. You always said life was about experiences and finding your purpose in life. I have come to find mine. I love you both, James x> *Send*

He had to clear his head from his hangover haze and his conflicting emotions, the guilt tore at his stomach as he kept thinking about his aunty and how much she would be worrying. He ran along the beach for several kilometres before he stopped to catch his breath, looking over to his side he watched as a family were playing in the sand. It reminded him of how he had played with his mother and father when he was a boy. He shook his head and turned around making once again for the beach hut. Having showered and dressed he walked up to find Lotte stood there in her apron serving a customer. She smiled broadly and waved at him as he walked up to find a table.

'Good morning, James.' She lay a menu on his table and bit her lip. Her long curly hair was tied up today, showing more of her beautiful face.

'Lotte, our evening together was amazing. I wanted to say how much I enjoyed it, thank you.' He said as his cheeks reddened. 'Are you free tonight?' he asked hopefully.

Over the next two days James and Lotte spent time together, walking, swimming and dining. On the fourth evening as the sun set, she walked him to the door of his hired beach hut accommodation. He unlocked the hut door and gestured for her to go inside of the dark hut. She looked back up to the dune bank to check her father or relatives were not watching them as she entered. She threw her shawl onto the two-seater sofa and turned back to James, her face half in shadow but he could still see her beautiful smile. 'James, I…' she started as a noise behind her made her freeze before she screamed loudly as a huge dark figure came out of the shadows and rushed towards them. On hearing the scream Lotte's father ran down from the bar to see what had happened.

At the exact same moment James rushed in pushing Lotte aside as he swung hard for the tall dark figure. The figure caught his arm mid swing and sent James flying hard against the wall winding him, his chest tight and ripping with what felt like broken glass with every breath. Lotte's father entered and grabbed his daughter pulling her outside to safety as other people started gathering outside the beach hut. Torches and mobile phones lit up to see the cause of the commotion.

James quickly stood gritting his teeth to find the figure standing over him. The figure was easily six foot six tall and heavily set but with a ripped athletic build. James took a fighting stance and edged forward as the figure held his arms up in submission 'James… wait.' The deep South-African voice said.

Lotte's father put an arm inside to turn the huts' light on, as James and the stranger both winced in the fluorescent bulbs light. Before them stood a middle-aged pale skinned male of mixed race descent, he had a scar on one eyebrow and a squint nose that appeared to have been smashed many times. But it was his eyes that made him appear menacing. They were large, jet black and cold. He wore black cargo trousers and military boots; his large muscular chest was squeezed into a dark-grey Armani t-shirt that tightened over his bulging large biceps.

'Lotte? Are you okay?' spat James desperately half-turning to check she was safe.

'James…' repeated the large South-African, stepping forward.

'Who are you?' asked James, eyeing the stranger up and down, his fists still clenched tightly. 'How do you know who I am?'

'I am Jared Bruce, your uncle Max asked me to come looking for you.'

Said the giant, 'I also knew your father Andrew… He was a good bloke.'

James lowered his arms and rubbed his shoulder where he had collided with the wall moments earlier. He turned to Lotte and her father and gave them a smile. 'It is okay, I know this man.'

'It is not okay…' shouted Lotte's father irately as he held his daughter back, eyeing the large trespasser. 'I want no trouble here. You both must go, now!'

'Lotte, I…' started James but her father ushered her away and turned her back towards the bar.

'You have 10 minutes. Get out.' Her father retorted before storming off back to the restaurant after his daughter.

James turned again to Jared and slumped onto the sofa. 'Well thank you for that.'

Jared said nothing but pulled out the large kit bag containing the scuba gear and placed it on the small dining table between them. 'I think you have some explaining to do young man…'

Chapter 5

The New Job

Amsterdam Centraal Station, Amsterdam.

James and Jared sat on the 009369 Thalys train as it promptly arrived at the Amsterdam Centraal Train Station.

'You have some balls mate.' Laughed Jared as the train stopped at the terminal. 'I would never have attempted a crossing like that.' He laughed again as he shook his head. 'Your uncle will be arriving first thing tomorrow morning to collect you. So, for now let us go to the hotel and keep out of trouble, eh.'

James lifted his bags and followed the large man off the train. During their 42-minute train journey Jared had explained that his job was locating people that did not want to be found. When James' uncle had called asking if he could look into any European interactions James may have made it took him only two days to find him.

'Hull is famous for two things…' started Jared, with his index finger up, 'Being unbelievably boring and two,' he said raising another finger, 'It has the P&O to Rotterdam used by perverts, Stag and Hen parties and stoners. Since your passport states that you are still inside the UK, I could only assume you chose the clandestine approach.'

'Very clever…' replied James. Honestly impressed. 'And the hut?'

'So, I did some groundwork along the Rotterdam / Monster beachfront, and low and behold, there you were flirting with the pretty barmaid.' Jared lit a cigarette and laughed again, his dark eyes piercing James' as he spoke. 'I called your uncle, telling him where you were. He told me to find out what you were doing. So, I broke into your hut and searched your belongings. And here we are.'

'I don't want to go back to England.' Spat James indignantly. 'I wanted to see the world, have some experiences and live a little. Say, Jared. What do you actually do here in Amsterdam?' asked James.

'As *Kylie* once said… '*Better the Devil you know*', mate.'

Jared frog marched him all the way to the entrance of the Waldorf Astoria Amsterdam on Herengracht in the beating heart of the amazing canal labyrinthine city. The hotel was set into a terrace of beautiful buildings that ran the entire length of the canal. The detailed stepped entrance sat between two parallel windows that were mirrored either side and above for each additional floor. A Juliet balcony sat above the entrance and housed a central banner flagpole that flittered in the warm summer breeze. The dark blue and ivory text Waldorf Astoria Amsterdam rippled ever so elegantly.

Jared eyed the street before he entered, James tried to see what he could see but only saw hotel clients, tourists and locals milling about. They walked in through the luxurious entrance hall to the decadent interior of highly polished marble and soft lighting. The furniture was antique and truly breath-taking, let alone the magnificent artwork that honoured the walls. James followed Jared to the reception where he began a conversation in Dutch. James quickly decided to walk around the reception area and keep himself entertained. He noticed two Chinese males both dressed in expensive black suits stood to one side watching Jared closely, they hadn't noticed him, but he thought it best to steer clear of them. Jared had finished and beckoned James over. Walking over to the impressive elevator they soon arrived on the second floor. Jared remained silent until he had opened the room door, checked the corridor, entered first checking every side room, under the bed and windows before he gave James a nod that everything was all in order. This made James feel a little uneasy.

'Are we expecting anyone?' he asked playfully, but Jared just glared with his dark cold eyes.

'Stay inside and wait for your uncle in the morning.' barked Jared.

'Do you want to get something to eat?' asked James.

'You can explore the canals with Max tomorrow. My job here is done. Order room service if you want something now.' Jared left the room key on a side console table and walked to the door.

'You know I actually came to Amsterdam to look for you, after how much my uncle used to talk about you. I was going to ask if you could help me out with finding a job and somewhere to stay.' said James hopefully with a small smile.

'Pleasure meeting you kiddo.' replied Jared, as he left the room, closing the door behind him.

James walked over to a window and watched as Jared left swiftly making a left out of the hotel towards the Amstel River. James watched idly as several boats came and went from either direction, but what caught his eye as he looked down were the two Chinese men in dark suits that began to follow Jared. James started banging furiously on the windowpane, but it was no good. Jared could not hear him. He looked around the room at his phone, then the key on the console table. He grabbed both and ran out of the room making his way to the reception then the foyer.

He slid down the steps in his haste and began running along the canal side towards the Amstel. He looked either way and saw the two Chinese men crossing the Blauwbrug and just ahead of them was Jared, oblivious of their presence. James ran after them across the 19th-century bridge that traversed over the Amstel River. Tourists were taking pictures of the views and city landmarks. He passed the impressive white blocked frame and burnt orange roof of the National Opera & Ballet theatre. As Jared and his pursuers turned right at the next bridge beside a large black slab called the Joods Verzetsmonument or Monument to Jewish Resistance.

He cleared the corner at speed and was now only fifty metres behind the Chinese men, Jared was a clear fifty metres ahead of them as he entered the Rembrandt House Museum further up the street.

"Where are you going..." James thought to himself. On arriving at the entrance to the 17th-century house where Rembrandt lived & worked for 20 years, he saw that there was a special viewing taking place that meant the museum was open longer than normal. But it would cost €30 to enter.

He paid the old man at the desk so he could enter, then began looking for Jared amongst the crowds. In a small side room, he could see several chairs leant up against the wall beneath the many works of Rembrandt. He was shocked at how powerful the vivid forms and expert contrasts of light and shadow within each painting were; he understood what made Rembrandt hold the title of a Master. He turned into a quitter room where he saw one of the Chinese men stood up close to Jared, it appeared that they were hugging. James wanted to call out but stopped himself when he saw Jared withdraw a huge hunting knife from the Chinese man's rib cage. The ten-inch blade would have easily severed the man's heart. Jared turned to half drag the now deceased pursuer over to one of the chairs and sat him down in it tilting his head back and closing his eyes. To a bystander he looked simply asleep in the chair. Tired of viewing all the artwork.

Jared's cold dark eyes flicked up at movement in the archway, James had moved quickly to hide in the other room, but he was not quick enough. Jared stalked closer towards him, knife in hand as the other Chinese man appeared and charged at him, knocking the knife away and sending them both flying onto the chessboard black and white marble floor of the museum.

James stole a look through the doorway as the two men grappled violently on the floor; dozens of violent blows were being dealt by both parties, but they did not seem to stop.

James saw the Chinese man grab the knife before he pushed it slowly towards Jared's exposed neck. James leapt into action grabbing one of the wooden chairs and struck the suited man hard from behind sending him heavily to the floor. Jared stood touching his neck where the blade had nicked him. But then his strong arm and hand, held a vice-like grip around James neck as he pushed him against the wall.

'What are you doing here boy?' he spat aggressively.

'These two men followed you from the hotel… I came to warn you.'

Whimpered James.

Jared rubbed his bruised jaw. 'I saw them watching me when I was at the reception, and then when I left…' he shook his head as he looked at the two bodies before them. 'I didn't need your help kiddo.'

'Your neck is bleeding heavily. Use this…' said James handing over a handkerchief.

'Go back to the hotel James. Forget what you just saw and do not come back here. Understood!'

Jared watched James run outside before he went back into the room.

One of the side doors opened as a slim man in his late fifties entered. He wore a cool pale linen suit and a Fedora hat. And was flanked by two large bald-headed men in matching dark suits, matching earpieces and stern angry expressions.

'Our organisation does not permit failures. Monsieur Araignée.' The man clicked his finger as one of the bald men took out a silenced Glock 17, he cocked it but then handed it to Jared with a simple nod. The large bald man then walked to and closed the entrance door before locking it.

The Chinese man who had been hit with the chair began to stir on the floor as he looked up to see the four men standing over him. Jared pulled up the pistol, before shooting the Chinese man twice in the face. The silenced 'thut thut' echoed in the small room as the spent casings tinged on the black and white chessboard floor.

'Who was that child?' the fedora man demanded, 'Bring him here now!'

'He is nobody sir. He will be leaving Amsterdam first thing tomorrow.' Replied Jared hotly.

'The child has heard and seen far too much, Monsieur Araignée.' muttered the Fedora man.

'He will not tell a soul.' Answered Jared. 'I can personally vouch for him.'

'Indeed… Monsieur Araignée. You will shoot him tonight!" spat the Fedora man.

'Ring Ring' a muffled phone began to ring from somewhere in the room, 'Ring Ring'

'It is *Number One*, sir.' said one of the bald men, answering his phone. 'Yes sir.' The bald man hung up the phone and turned to Fedora. '*Number One* wishes to meet the young boy.'

The man in the Fedora turned to look at Jared 'Bring him in.' then up at the CCTV camera in the corner of the room before giving a slight bow. He retreated back through the side door that he entered through followed by his two henchmen.

Jared half walked and half ran back to the hotel and up the second floor. He knocked on the door with three hard bangs and it was opened immediately by James.

Jared looked him in the eyes with his cold dark stare but said nothing for some time. He stood with his hands over his mouth breathing heavily.

'Why didn't you stay inside the hotel James?' he asked quietly.

'I told you, those two men.' He started. 'I had to try and warn you.'

Jared rubbed his eyes and gritted his teeth. 'My employer watched what happened inside the museum.' On seeing James's lost expression he continued, 'He has access to the security cameras in the majority of buildings in Amsterdam. He saw what you did to help me… And now he wants to meet you.' he said reluctantly.

'Why does he want to meet me?' asked James hesitantly.

'For tea and biscuits James, what the blerrie hell do you think?' shouted Jared sarcastically.

'This organisation is involved in some dark kak and these people are ruthless. I mean drugs, prostitution, arms trafficing and some other things I will tell you about after your eighteenth birthday.'

'Do you think they want to kill me?' asked James taken aback by it all.

'Nah kiddo,' huffed Jared as he kicked the table making everything on top shudder, 'If they wanted you dead you and me would not be having this conversation.' He paced again before screaming in frustration. 'Ahh!! You know it took me two years to be asked to meet him. Two fokken years of nasty, degrading and brutal kak. You managed a face to face within an hour of being in Amsterdam.'

'Are you jealous?' spat James playfully.

Jared crossed the room like an irate bull charging a red flag as he grabbed James by the shoulders, lifting him off the ground. 'This isn't a blerrie joke kiddo! My employer is not the *normal* type of boss. He will ask you to surrender all and follow orders without hesitation. He deals death with every sentence and takes whatever he wants, whenever he wants. This is not a world that a 14-year-old child should witness!!' Spat Jared more than angry.

'I don't think this is something you should be shouting about Jared. You don't want the entire hotel to hear this do you?' called James awkwardly holding a finger to his lip.

'The rooms are soundproofed.' He replied as he began pacing the room. 'Bliksem!' he shouted as he gripped the backrest of a nearby dining chair causing the wood to creak under the immense pressure under his white knuckles. 'Have you heard of Pandora's Box?' he spat irritably. James just nodded silently.

'Well the organisation I work for and represent makes Pandora's Box look like a shoebox full of fluffy kittens. Leave your phone here, and come with me.'

Jared walked out of the hotel with James swiftly following him. Jared had given James pointers of what to do, what to say and more importantly what not to say. They crossed several bridges before they came to a terraced row of buildings opposite the Hortus Botanicus Amsterdam, a picturesque compact botanical garden.

James could see security cameras all along the street that seemed to watch and follow him and Jared as they approached a large fronted building that appeared to be vacant offices. Jared knocked on a large door that opened to a narrow corridor and three large men in matching dark suits. They nodded and let them inside, as one spoke into a wrist communicator announcing their arrival. They walked through to the back of the building of what appeared to be offices in rooms that once made up the original grand house's interior. The grand fireplaces and finer architectural features were all still in place but the rooms had been recarpeted and filled with dozens of ergonomic desks and swivel chairs.

They came to another large door that was opened as they approached. Again, CCTV cameras watched their every move. As they entered this smaller room James noticed that the windows were boarded up and no cameras were visible inside or further along the corridors. Across from them was an old wooden elevator encased in an outer rusted black metal cage that looked like its prime was during the 1800's. Next to it stood a shiny steel elevator door, the modern upgrade. Jared pushed the button and the door slid open silently. They entered and stood there until the door closed and the elevator began to drop. Approximately 20 seconds later the door slid open revealing a huge brightly

lit chamber. With dozens of small offices coming off along two of the side walls. Ahead of them was a laboratory with several technicians, males and females dressed in long white lab coats using all manner of unknown machines and stirred test tubes and beakers filled with different chemicals. On the last wall was a single door that was closed and guarded by two bald-headed men, and this was where they were headed. As James crossed the open plan chamber, he saw that each of the offices bore a small brass plaque reading different cities around the world. Moscow, Rome, Hong Kong, New York, London and many others.

The two of them stood outside the main door as one of the bald men frisked Jared. And removed the large hunting knife and his mobile phone. The large man then turned to James before looking back to Jared with a lost expression. Jared nodded and the large man frisked James too. He smiled as he stood back, 'One seldom sees a child without their mobile phone,' sneered the large bald-headed man before he ordered them through the door.

The room beyond was cavernous in itself, roughly one-hundred-foot square. The centre of the room was filled with a large conference table flanked by very expensive Fritz Hansen egg chairs in black leather and chrome bases. The head of the table held a more tactical looking Alpha Command Chair which had monitors on either arm with a sleek buttoned keyboard panel on a collapsible metal arm. The far end of the room also held another more traditional looking writing desk of solid wood. Behind this stood an ornate office chair that looked largely uncomfortable to James. To the side of this desk, he could see a small recess that transpired to be another door as it opened shortly after they had entered the room.

A tall female entered the room, she was slender yet powerful looking and had a stare that matched Jared's for its intensity. She carried her dark hair up and tight in a rear bun. She wore a dark red trouser suit combo and flat shoes; heels were definitely not needed as she was already over six feet tall. She walked in and sat behind the old writing desk and ushered them both over.

James suddenly had the same feeling he got when he had been stood in front of his Head Dean back at Fettes. The female was German by her accent although her English was impeccable. She looked over to Jared and barked 'Report' at him before she opened a manilla folder that lay on her desk. Jared started relaying the events of the two Chinese males following him and how he *disposed* of them in the Rembrandt Museum. She did not speak at all, she just glared at him indignantly as she tapped her pen impatiently on the file on the desk. 'And you?' she snapped looking at James. 'Where do you come into all of this?'

'He is a friend's nephew…' started Jared before he was cut short.

'I asked him…' she spat crossly, holding up her index finger to silence him.

She looked at James and scowled. 'List your attributes…' she started as she began looking through the folder in front of her.

James stood speechless for a moment taking in what was happening, he looked to Jared who simply raised an eyebrow in response. Then James took a deep breath and started speaking. 'I am an orphan. I am observant. I can speak French and German fluently and was told that I am likely to get a First in Oriental languages. I can ski to a professional level, and I am an expert marksman with a rifle and shotgun. I have studied martial arts since I was six years old, and I know how to fight dirty and get the job done.' He said, raising his chin confidently.

'Anything else?' retorted the female, unimpressed not even looking up at him.

'I hate tea, it's the bloody reason for the downfall of the British Empire. I am partial to a good strong black coffee.' He said with a smile as Jared shook his head in disbelief. 'Much like yourself, Ma'am.'

She dropped her pen and eyeballed him hard from across the desk. Then unexpectedly she smiled and laughed aloud. 'And how... Young man, do you know that I like strong coffee?'

'Like I said... I'm observant.' He replied assertively, trying a cheeky smile.

The tall female stood and held out a hand for him to shake, 'I am and will only be referred to as Number Two or Ma'am. And what pray tell are we to call you? Mr?'

'Bond... James Bond.' He said, accepting her proffered hand.

'*Number One* wished to see you, and I must honestly say that he appears to be impressed.' She looked over their shoulders at the man standing behind them.

James and Jared both turned with a start at the unexpected arrival of the man now standing behind them.

The man had crept up behind them and made no sound at all whilst they had been talking to Number Two. The man looked Eastern European but had pale grey eyes that shot right through you. He was clean shaven and very well groomed; his eyebrows were so faint and pale they looked shaved adding to his menacing glare. His suit was visibly tailored, and he held himself with a confidence that exudes power. His most distinct feature was a large scarred deep indentation near his left temple. The man spoke softly and slowly but with a passion of a dictator addressing his people.

'Orion is much more than a multi-billion pound organisation. It is a living and breathing organism that operates for the brotherhood of man. We take action where world governments fail or are hindered by too much bureaucracy and the limitations surrounding the human rights of terrorists and war criminals.' The man stepped between them raising his arm as though to point at Number Two. 'I trust in two things Mr Bond, loyalty and success. I have no tolerance for failure or betrayal.' His accent was indecipherable, he sounded English but had so many influencing and changeable phonetics that James could not be certain where this man was from. 'I seldom like surprises or the unexpected and therefore must test loyalty… Mr Bond.' He nodded to Number Two who had pulled out a Colt .45 revolver from the desk and placed it in front of Jared.

'Kill him Monsieur Araignée!' he said effortlessly. His stone face did not even flinch.

Jared took the gun off the desk, raised it and pulled back the hammer placing it at the back of James bowed head, James could feel the cold hard barrel as Jared pushed it harder against his head.

'Sorry kiddo…' said Jared as he squeezed the trigger. '*Click*' The chamber was empty.

James juddered as his breath failed him, he suddenly felt like he was going to vomit as his hands and legs began to shake.

Number One simply smiled. 'I trust in loyalty… I test loyalty… Now Mr Bond, kindly take the gun and shoot Number Two in the face.' He said coldly, nodding across the desk.

Number Two shot a scared look at the three men standing across from her. 'Was!! Sie können nicht ernst sein!' she shouted in horror. 'Du Bastard!!' shouted Number Two in German, her face ashen with shock taking a step backwards.

Jared handed him the gun and whispered morosely as he closed his eyes shaking his head, 'He will take everything from you kiddo.'

James' hand shook with fear as he raised the heavy handgun, pointed it at the tall destitute female and he squeezed the trigger. 'Click' The chamber was again empty.

The tall German woman's face returned instantly to composure and resolve as she started clapping slowly. 'Welcome to Orion Mr Bond.' Number Two had acted the victim very well. James could have sworn she really had no idea that she was about to be shot. James dropped the gun back onto the desk as Jared placed a hand on his shoulder. 'This is the initiation, James.' Whispered Jared. 'And you just passed it. May God have mercy on your soul mate.' Jared walked away and out of the large conference room leaving James standing with *Number One* and *Number Two*.

'You will begin processing immediately and then if you are again successful, full training.' Started Number Two as she closed the folder on her desk. 'Do you have any questions?'

James didn't really know what to do or say so kept his mouth shut and shook his head.

'You will be met outside by one of our resource operatives, they will ask you some questions. Answer them honestly and without hesitation.' Said Number Two authoritatively. 'Then you will be taken for a physical examination. Leave now.'

James quickly made his way back to the doorway where Jared had just left and closed it before catching his breath. His heart had been pounding the entire time, but he had managed to keep a cool facade…

until now. His hands shook uncontrollably, and his entire body began to sweat. The adrenaline from him having a gun pointed at his head to him pointing a gun at a stranger's face had taken its toll. He was about to vomit all over his shoes when Jared pulled him to the side away from the two bald sentry guards. 'Toilets are this way kiddo.' He called as he dragged James away.

Back inside the main operations room *Number One* smiled a sinister smile. 'A high functioning, educated orphan… It would appear we have the makings of a traditional British Spy.' *Number One* laughed maniacally as he watched James leaving with Jared on the monitor of his Alpha command chair.

James bent over a stall as he retched up a second time. His hands still shook violently, and he felt utterly exhausted. Jared stood behind him with his hands crossed looking down at him sternly.

'I told you they would make you do something like this.' He said, shaking his head. 'Now you are in their pocket… What the bloody hell am I going to tell your uncle Max in the morning eh?'

James stood back up and flushed the chain, taking several pieces of tissue to wipe his mouth and chin of the debris before throwing them into the swirling basin. 'We tell him the truth. Or you call him now and tell him, save him a wasted journey.' James walked over to beside Jared and washed his hands and face. The cold water aided him in returning to a semblance of normality.

'You want me to tell Max that I unknowingly signed his 14-year-old nephew up to a life in the Dutch criminal underworld… He will break my *Blerrie* neck.'

James looked at Jared in the large mirror that ran the entire bathroom wall. 'You know something…' he started. 'Today… at the museum… was the first time in a long time that I actually felt alive.'

'Yeah, well trust me… The novelty soon wears off…' replied Jared again shaking his head. 'Come on… You don't want to keep them waiting.'

They left the toilets to find a middle-aged female in a long blue ankle dress and matching blazer waiting for them in the chamber. She had a pretty face and thick glasses that made her green eyes look massive through the lens. She held a metal clipboard in her hand and gave a small bow. 'Come with me.' She led James into one of the small offices that ran the length of the chamber room. She sat at a simple white desk and tapped several keys on a slim monitored computer bringing the dark screen to life. James could see the blue and white screen reflected in the large lenses of her glasses but did not want to appear to be staring at her, so he looked to the walls of the office. The three walls were smooth and painted a plain white, they had no interior decoration, no furniture, paintings or fittings. She beckoned for James to sit opposite her as she opened the metal clipboard taking out three documents, all stapled at the top left.

She placed them in between them on the white desk and began reading out the questions written on them. As James answered she in turn filled the empty boxes adjacent with his answer. Every now and then she would turn to the monitor and click several keys. Her large eyes darted this way and that across the large monitor screen.

James was there for what seemed like an hour before she abruptly stood up and placed the three completed documents back inside the metal clipboard. 'Time for your Physical.' She pointed to a door on the other side of the chamber.

James had imagined the physical would take part in a uber high-tech lab with ventilators and running machines, but the corridor emerged into a small dojo similar to the one he had learnt his discipline in as a younger child. He looked around at the wooden weapons adorning the walls and the target manikins dotted around the edge of the padded floor in the centre. He was alone in the room, so he began to walk the edge admiring the large variety of weaponry on display. Some wooden, some sparing and some razor sharp and very much lethal.

"*Stand in the centre.*" Called a nondescript voice over a tannoy speaker secreted in the ceiling.

James stood for two minutes in silence before a sliding door opened on his right to reveal four men and three women in white Dobok suits. They all hurriedly walked up to him and took a basic left foot stance shouting a kiup in unison that filled and echoed around the room, 'Yah!'

"Oh no…" he thought to himself, taking in the situation developing around him.

The physical examination transpired to be a test to see how he could manage against several opponents. These were not teenagers that he was used to, and they looked angry at his audacity to challenge them in their dojo.

'Good evening.' He smiled at their stern and aggressive faces. 'You know… something in your body language tells me you're not the talkative type.' He said as the first three moved quickly towards him. 'Okay then,' he shuffled a step back as he raised his guard in preparation.

Two men and a female encircled him instantly as he held his guard, his cautious eyes scanning their hands and feet as they moved in tighter. He had assumed that they would knock him about a bit to test his technique and stamina… he was wrong. The aggressive adults he now faced had no intention of going soft on him as they applied each and every kick and punch in the style of full competition contact. He discovered this very quickly as each of his attackers landed very heavy blows to his torso and one to his left leg making him wince.

'Right…' he said aloud. 'Time to shine' he told himself as he blocked the smaller of the three and grabbed her leg following her high kick. 'Let's do this.' He said as he elbowed the female hard above her knee making her cry out. 'Figure 4 Toehold' he said more to himself as he raised his right leg dragging her foot to his hip, his left arm slipped underneath her foot as his right hand pushed down on her toes causing her to squeal out loud as the tendons ripped apart. The two males moved in together with a bombardment of volleys, so he used the female as a human shield twisting her raised leg so that she was always in between him and them.

It didn't take them long to get bored of this as they called two more over to assist. He now had five adults to contend with.

James took a moment to catch his breath and in doing so his mind flashed back to his own dojo where he saw himself as a six year old bowing to the sensei. Jiu Jitsu was perfect for quick and effective takedowns, but he had always questioned his teacher why the proposed attacker was always rubbish at fighting and meant to just stand there and take his blows or allow them to be put into holds. As a reward for his inquisitive question his teacher had ensured the 'attacker' would always be a master. Meaning one of two results, he learnt quickly or bled quickly.

Another loud kiup brought him quickly back to his five attackers in the basement dojo of an Amsterdam crime syndicate. He exhaled and readied himself as the three men and two women now circled him, like sharks around a whale cub. He realised that he had to start dropping some of them if he wanted to survive. The attackers took it in turns to kick,

slap and punch at him intermittently, so he had to keep his eyes all over the place. He quickly noticed a pattern in their attacks, a sequence that repeated different moves but the same attacker. "Bingo" he thought. As the next punch came in towards him, he twisted himself so that he ended up almost on top of the attacker, using a wide elbow block he used his other fist to strike the throat of the now exposed male. This as you'd imagine worked very well. He then turned quickly as the next attacker in the sequence standing behind him raised his leg to strike James's back, again he moved into the attack sweeping the incoming leg upward before following through with his own powerful kick to the side of the stranger's knee cap. After a devastating crunch the man dropped holding his knee as he rolled in agony. "Two down…" he thought. One of the females landed a hard punch to his ribs that made him call out in agony as he absorbed the impact. His back was still very bruised from his ordeal beneath the cargo vessel and this sucker punch just woke all the old bruises up.

He marked her and went to stop the next move in the sequence, oddly enough the attackers still continued in their methodological approach. James anticipated the move just by looking at the attacker, his confidence grew as he managed to take another male down with a right punch to their temple and a swift wristlock – "Mao de Vaca" that would take a very long time to heal. His audacity overtook him as he gave a cheeky smile. Things were looking up for him and he was relishing the contact sport that he so dearly missed from his childhood. The buzz one got from sparring, from the endorphin chemical released from full contact sports.

Bang – he was forcibly and aggressively blindsided by the two others still on the edge of the mats. He hadn't anticipated them joining in at that very moment. As the two new attackers lifted him off his feet he grabbed the collar of one of their Dobok suits and lifted his knee to the side of their face as they began their descent onto the mats. His knee was forced upward with the impact of hitting the ground, causing the attacker to absorb the full impact into his jaw, knocking him out instantly. The other attacker though was already on his feet and kicking at James's now foetal body on the ground.

James took several kicks from either side as the remaining three attackers. Two females and the new male laid into him, winding him badly. Every breath was now like broken glass in his lungs. He had to get up quick or he wouldn't be able to take much more of this. As one of the females re-chambered her leg to kick again, he rolled into her grounded shin, locking his leg around her other raised leg. Kicking up hard and straight right into her groin sending her up and backward. He flipped up as the last male ran at him, ducking to the left he raised his right leg to kick the man in the stomach, before spinning around to kick him again with his left leg, this time to the groin. The male doubled over as James moved in to stand by his side. A heavy blow to the back of the neck sent the man down hard. He grappled the man on the floor and taking his lapels he placed the man into a Thrust choke.

James straightened his top as he rolled the choked-out man onto the mat and looked at the last female across from him. The other female he had just kicked was beginning to stand so he made his move. Jumping off the back of the man with a broken knee he tore through the air with his leg coiled. As he neared the standing female, he released his kick sending her backward several paces. She could see what he had intended as she anticipated it easily enough. But this wasn't his goal. He landed next to the other female who was on her knees about to stand, he raised his leg horizontally and dropped it quickly leg unbent as his heel kicked her hard in the back of her head knocking her out cold. 'One left…' he said smugly as six of the seven attackers either lay unconscious or were rolling around in agony on the floor.

The female shook her head in disbelief and walked over to the side of the dojo, taking a long Kendo sword off the wall as she spun it several times in her hand with great precision and mastery. She took a defensive stance and moved forward towards James.

She swung the wooden sword at his head causing him to duck quickly, then across towards his torso. He tried to block the long sword, but the hard edge nearly broke his lower arm. He tucked his injured arm in and took several paces backward. He heard his uncle's voice inside his head, "*The greatest weapon you have is the one your opponent doesn't know you have.*"

He smiled and turned his back on the sword wielding female as he unclipped his thick belt buckle. She ran at him screaming with the sword held high in the air as he pulled out the belt with one hand, ducking quickly as he swung the belt around into her face, his heavy buckle making hard contact with her lips. She stood in shock as her lips opened revealing a cascade of fresh red blood all down her white Dobok. She raised a shaking hand to her ravaged lips as she looked at him. James wrapped the belt in both hands creating a taught length between them as he moved in towards her. He had studied Jujitsu and other martial arts since he was a young child, but the combat art he liked most was the special forces training his uncle Max had given him. The art of using whatever was to hand in the most devastating way. The injured female raised the wooden sword again, as she swung it left and right trying to take off his head. He just waited, blocked and ducked until she overstretched, then wrapped the belt around her arms, tightening it forcing her hands and wrists to pull together. In a flash of movement, he pushed her own hands backwards still holding the long sword hard into her face as the sword hit her forehead knocking her back. He did this again as she dropped the sword. She attempted to take his legs out with a powerful Muay Thai sweep kick. He knew if he tried to block this devastating kick with his already weakened arm it would most likely result in broken bones. He had to try and take her off balance.

James ran at the woman with everything he had pushing her backwards and off to the side away from her kicking leg. The woman fell backwards, tripping on one of her fellow fallen attackers as James fell on top of her. James straddled her and grabbed both her forearms still wrapped in the belt.

'My mother always said never to hit a woman…' said James, 'But technically, I'm not actually hitting you, am I?' He pushed her arms hard and fast several times as she once again hit herself in the face. Her eyes began glazing over from the repeated hard impacts. James felt a hard kick from the side as one of the downed fighters managed to inflict one final kick before rolling over limp and unconscious. The female rolled onto her knees as she raised her bound hands up over James' head under his chin making his head tip back. James could feel the thick leather of his belt pressing against his throat cutting off the blood and oxygen as she applied a rear naked choke hold. The female mounted behind him like a human backpack or turtle shell with her legs wrapped around his chest, her knees high under his armpits, her feet holding his legs open and useless.

His free hands squeezed at her wrists, his thumb joints burning as he applied as much pressure as he could so she would loosen her grip on his neck. She screamed with rage as James threw an elbow into her ribs with one arm then an elbow at her chin with the other arm, but her grip just became stronger the more he wriggled. He clenched his fist into a tight ball as he placed it against her cheek, he then slapped hard and fast with his open hand pushing her cheeks together, this angered her as she screamed in a foreign tongue. James loosened his fist sliding out his middle finger knuckle so that it protruded out ever so slightly, he then held it against her temple and punched with his other hand sending her head into his protruding knuckle. Her eyes rolled up after the second blow, her legs went limp, and her grip slackened. James pulled her arms forward freeing his neck as he inhaled deeply filling his lungs with fresh burning air. One more swift elbow caught her chin and she fell on her side.

James grabbed the wooden kendo sword from behind them and raised it high above his head ready to strike down as she looked up at him, anger filled her eyes, but she could not do anything, she was at his mercy. James relaxed his grip on the sword, lowering it to his waist before dropping it to the floor, letting her go. He untied the belt and walked back to the centre of the dojo before bowing to all of the seven incapacitated attackers.

The tannoy speaker above him rang out once more making him look up, "*Congratulations Mr Bond.*"

It was the unmistakable German voice of Number Two.

The next day Jared arrived at the hotel early to ensure James was up and ready. He looked at his face and laughed. 'You survived the physical then?'

'Thank you for warning me about that Jared…' replied James wincing as he put on his shirt. He looked down at his bruised arms and the large bruises along his back and side from the previous night.

'You're the one who wanted to dance with the Devil kiddo.' He laughed as he helped himself to some of the toast that sat on the hotel room dining table. 'Besides, you will heal quickly enough. Live today, die tomorrow.'

James looked up suddenly, his mind racing. 'My father used to say that… Those very words.' James walked over to Jared and looked him in the eye. 'Yesterday, when we were back at the beach hut, you said that you knew my father… How did you know him?'

Jared's cold eyes squinted as he recoiled inside, but he remained silent. He walked over to the window of the apartment suite and looked out at the boats moving slowly along the dark waters of the canal below. He turned back to James and nodded.

'Okay… Your uncle Max and I worked together for many years. He saved my neck dozens of times and likewise I saved his. During one of our missions, we needed an extra pair of hands for a logistical matter. Your uncle called in your father Andrew.'

James stood dumbstruck, in all his years with his uncle he had never been told that his father had run a mission with him. Jared continued, 'We needed someone to carry something out of the middle-east and into England. Your father managed this undertaking via his connections through work, and thus our partnership began… You know he worked for Vickers as an armaments company representative. He arranged for millions of tonnes of ammunition, firearms, armoured steel and military ship parts to be transported all around the globe. So, your uncle and I persuaded him to include some specialist items into these shipments.'

James was agog at hearing this, 'You're telling me that my father was a smuggler? What was it? Drugs? WMDs?' he spat in outrage.

Jared walked over to calm him down as the buzzer on the telephone rang out. Jared walked over to answer it. On hearing the receptionist, he turned to James holding up a finger to silence his rants.

'Your uncle Max has just arrived and is heading up.' He said, replacing the handset into its wall mounted cradle.

James fell silent as he finished buttoning his shirt. He rubbed his mouth as a distraction, his mind racing of what to say to his uncle. He felt uncomfortably nervous, more so than he did during yesterday's initiation. It is odd, he thought, how certain members of your own family have such power over you. Three loud bangs on the door made them both look at each other, James was uncertain who looked more concerned as Jared made his way to the door.

Max was a large man, barrel chested and broad shouldered, he still carried the arms of a weightlifter and the belly of a stalwart drinker. He stood six inches shorter than Jared, but James knew it would be a tough battle between these two old lions. They stared at each other across the threshold before Jared moved aside to let him in. Max walked into the room and stood before James and frowned as he saw his battered nephew standing before him.

'Was this your handy work Jared?' spat Max, his thick Scottish accent echoing in the hotel room. He raised his chubby finger lifting James' bruised face. 'Well?'

'You know it wasn't me Max.' replied Jared hotly.

The two of them faced each other again and stood for a moment before Max's lip curled into a broad smile. 'Thank you for finding him before he got himself into too much trouble.' He embraced the larger man and patted his back as they both laughed. Max turned to James and raised an eyebrow.

'What were you playing at boy?' he scowled deeply, 'Your Aunty Charmian has been worried sick.' James knew too well that he too would have been worried but would not disclose this display of emotion.

James stood tall but remained silent.

'Quite a paper trial you left behind you…' he scoffed, shaking his head. 'The train ticket. The scuba gear… It didn't take me more than two hours to figure out what you'd done.' He walked over to James placing a hand on each of his shoulders. 'Damned reckless of you. Do you have any idea how bloody dangerous that was? Or how bloody illegal?' he scratched his head and paced the room. 'How we get you back is another matter.'

'I don't want to go back Max.' said James, finally speaking. 'I want to stay here.'

'And do what exactly?' his uncle laughed. 'No. You are coming back with me today.'

'That won't be possible as I already have a job.' Spat James, 'Tell him Jared.'

Jared looked up angrily, 'Oh you little-" he stepped forward shaking his head. 'Max…' he started awkwardly. 'James went to meet some people yesterday… From Orion.'

Max snapped around and punched Jared around the face knocking him onto the pristine white bed sheets. Then turned to James and slapped him with a back hand. Nowhere as hard as what Jared had received but it still hurt like hell.

'No!' he spat angrily, 'No way.' He shouted again. 'I will no' allow my wee nephew to be corrupted by that deranged organisation. I don't even want him associating with them, let alone acting as one of their hoodlum cronies.' He swore loudly and turned back to Jared, 'I've a right mind to shoot you for this. How could you let this happen Jared?'

Jared stood up rubbing his chin, his tongue checking around his gums for signs of blood. 'I didn't let anything happen Max… You know how this world works…' he said, stepping forward. 'You know better than anyone that you don't just walk away, not from them.'

Max turned on him again, this time his eyes were ablaze, James had never seen his uncle so irate before. 'Don't you dare.' Spat Max. 'Don't you dare…' he grabbed a chair from the small dining table and threw it against the wall. James had expected it to shatter into a thousand pieces but disappointedly it remained in one piece as it fell to the ground. Damn good quality furniture.

'My family has lost enough…' shouted Max tapping a sausage finger at Jared's chest, 'I have lost enough,' he moved his large finger to point at his own chest. He turned to James and stopped speaking. His eyes were red and full of tears. 'Why James…' he sobbed, 'Why them, why here of all places?'

Jared moved in between them and raised his hands to call for peace. 'It was an accident; James was in the wrong place at the wrong time. He followed me yesterday, he tried to help me, by saving my life when he saw two of Chen's hitmen follow me into a museum. Orion was watching our every move and he was brought in.'

Max poured himself a large drink from the crystal tumbler sat on the dresser, easily a triple serving.

Jared continued, 'You know what they would have done if I had refused...' he turned his head back to look at James. Max nodded sorrowfully at these words.

'You have sealed his fate, signed his death certificate, this wee boy... My bloody nephew!' he roared at Jared. 'How much do they know?' he calmed as he drank from his full glass.

'They know everything... Everything except who his father was or who you are.'

*

Chapter 6

The New Man

Barney's Coffeeshop, Haarlemmerstraat 102, 1013 EW, Amsterdam.

James stood in the window of the small coffee shop as he watched the hordes of tourists pass by outside. His uncle Max and Jared had been talking heatedly for hours in the back. He had been ordered to stay inside and not speak to or engage with anyone until they had finished. He turned back as two young men sat nearby who just sparked up a long joint. The pungent sickly-sweet aroma of cannabis filled the bar immediately, making James senses dull slightly. He walked towards the long bar that sat along the entire side of the narrow coffee shop. Behind the counter were shelves of merchandise for sale to tourists to prove they had visited the infamous Barney's. Baseball caps, cups, backpacks and bongs all lined up as if in any retail shop. The many tables that occupied the other wall of the narrow shop were filling up with tourists and locals alike. James ordered another large black coffee to counteract the pungent drug smoke filling his lungs and sat at the bar as the back room erupted in a verbal altercation.

'Bastard!' Max roared at Jared as he appeared through a small door from behind the counter. His uncle didn't look happy at all. His large face was red and flustered.

Some customers turned to see what the commotion was but on seeing Jared's large form walk out behind Max they soon turned back to their own business keeping their heads down. Max took James by the arms and held him close, his large arm squeezing his back in a tight embrace as he whispered something into his ear. He kissed the boy on the forehead and stormed out of the coffee shop alone.

Jared came to stand beside James and nodded to himself, 'Well he took that better than expected.'

Jared explained that Max would be travelling back to England alone that afternoon. Jared had agreed to watch over James and keep him safe until they could figure a way for him to get out of his new employ. Jared looked at James for a long moment before he brushed his shoulder gently. 'Are all your clothes like this?' he huffed and stood up, 'Come with me James.'

The afternoon was spent visiting the many haute couture stores along Amsterdam's Rodeo Drive, Bvlgari, Cartier, Louis Vuitton, Chanel, Burberry, Valentino and Tiffany & Co. James was astounded that Jared had credit accounts with each and every store and the staff not only knew him by name but treated him like a prince. This man was clearly connected.

Jared took James to his apartment along Leidseplein in central Amsterdam, the large property was a converted warehouse that had been furnished with several bedrooms, kitchen, equipped with a small gym, pool table and a room that was for the sole purpose of a walk-in wardrobe full of Jared's designer clothes. From the furnishings and décor Jared didn't have any children and no child had ever stepped foot inside the apartment. The set up oozed masculinity and was clearly a bachelor pad.

Jared spent most of his free time in his personal gymnasium within his apartment. When he'd finished he sat on one of the many sofas drinking cold beer watching television. Jared didn't ever say much, he was not the talkative or social type, but James was persistent and after a few days Jared began talking about himself. He had explained that he grew up in South Africa during the British / Apartheid Afrikaner government. His mother was Black, and his father was a White doctor, meaning that as a mixed-race male he was an outcast in all social reforms. The blacks saw him as a persona non grata and the whites saw him as a black man. School was tough in the segregationist communities against non-white citizens of South Africa and so were the streets of Johannesburg as someone who didn't belong or fit in on either side. Jared had left his family in Johannesburg at the age of 16 and joined the army, then the special forces. He had managed four years in the Légion étrangère or as it is informally known the French Foreign Legion of North Africa before he was discharged for assaulting a senior officer. He managed to work for other European militaries and governments where he had met James' uncle Max before he disappeared into the belly of Amsterdam's criminal underworld.

Jared walked around the canaled streets with James in tow as he explained who their employer was and what they actually did. Jared had advised that James was to shadow him for the first few weeks to see what was expected of him.

'Orion is a multinational organisation that manages the import and export of most of the world's drugs, weapons and anything else you can think of that governments and police forces want out of their country. But Orion is different in that they have a purpose. A purpose to actually help those world governments and police forces once and for all.'

Jared went on to explain that like any company there was a managerial structure. James had already met the people at the top, those two people that used the codes Number One and Number Two. Then there was senior management whose codes numbered between Three and Ten. Next came those using codes Eleven through to Fifty, Jared advised that nobody really saw who they were but they made everything work smoothly, he assumed they were officials and politicians but this was just his speculation. Then there were the lieutenants or the *enforcers* within Orion, Fifty to Eighty and this is what Jared was. He didn't disclose his number to James but just advised they did as instructed to ensure certain aspects of the company progressed without situation. Jared then went on to say that James was at the other end of the spectrum, down in the Three Hundreds somewhere. 'You work your way up, so they lower your number the higher your rank.'

'What number did you start at?' asked James.

'All I will say kiddo is that I worked blerrie hard to get where I am today. Orion, don't break people in gently James. They use you for their nefarious means then dispose of you should you fail or become weak or obstructive. We are basically buttons for them to press as and when required. This is akin to a fairy-tale world and we are the blerrie monsters that go bump in the night.' He paused as he looked up and down the street, all was quiet. 'You sure you want to enter this cold fokken world kiddo?' James swallowed hard and nodded.

Jared entered the small shop and walked to the back of the building telling James to wait outside the back room and watch the door, nobody was to come in or out. James could see a young Chinese male sat at a small Formica desk littered in printed papers and spreadsheets, who on seeing Jared's large figure enter the store went to stand up a move away, only for Jared to pull out a silenced Beretta 418 and shoot the man in the thigh with a quiet 'thut' dropping him to the floor taking half the paperwork off the desk.

'What is Chen doing back in Amsterdam?' spat Jared to the whimpering Chinese man.

'Please, Monsieur Araignée... I don't know anything. Please...' cried the Chinese man as he held his bloodied leg trying to stem the flow of blood.

'What is Chen doing back in Amsterdam?' Jared bent down in front of the injured man. 'I will not ask again.'

The injured man looked up and then back to his twitching leg, 'Okay, okay, just don't shoot me again Monsieur Araignée,' the man whimpered, 'Chen wants back in.' the man squealed as he winced in pain as he moved his leg.

'Where is he?' said Jared cooly with a raised eyebrow,

'The docks...' the injured man spat, 'Westpoort... He has men coming in every day via the Hong Kong cargo ships. He is accruing a small army.'

'How many are we talking about?' asked Jared, his intense dark eyes penetrating the injured Chinese man making him squirm as he sweat wildly, shock taking over him.

'I don't know... Nobody is allowed near the docks.' Whispered the bleeding man.

'Thank you.' Jared stood up and turned away, 'Now open the blerrie safe.'

The Chinese man did as he was told and opened the biometric safe revealing several plastic bags of white powder and a pale sandy colour, assumingly heroin and cocaine. But what Jared was after was the four large bundles of Euro notes at the back of the safe. He picked them up and with one of his large hands then turned back to the injured man. The Chinese man looked extremely pale and began to pass out on the floor.

'Tell Chen that we will not allow him to return, he has 12 hours to leave.' Spat Jared pocketing the money. He looked down to see the man was now unconscious as a blood pool began seeping out from beneath his thigh. 'Oh well, I will tell him myself.' He raised his pistol again and shot the man in the head before holstering his firearm and taking the remaining contents from the safe before locking it and walking back outside to find James still stood by the counter, oblivious.

Jared nodded to James who followed him outside, they turned the closed sign on the shop door around to display "*GESLOTEN*" and released the old locking mechanism built into the shop door as it slammed shut behind them.

'What happened in there?' asked James coyly, looking back to the closed office door, noticing the Chinese man hadn't come back out.

'I needed to leave a message.' Spat Jared coldly, pulling out his mobile as he dialled a number.

'Chen is back in town hiding at Westpoort Docks. He is building a small army and intends on muscling his way back in.' Jared listened then nodded 'uh-huh', 'Will do.' He hung up his phone and walked away, clicking his fingers at James for him to follow.

'You ever used a gun?' asked Jared as he purchased two bottles of water from a street vender.

'Rifle and shotgun many times, why?' replied James inquisitively.

'Come on...' replied Jared walking off again. 'Give me your phone.'

James opened his phone and passed it to Jared who quickly typed in an address and handed it back to James before taking out one of the large bundles of money he had taken from the dead Chinese man. James looked down at the address: Lijnbaansgracht 162/1, Club Kaliber.

'Take this.' said Jared handing over a small fortune in Euro notes, 'Go here and ask for Maria. Tell her that I sent you. She will look after you… Have fun kiddo.'

James arrived at the address displayed on his mobile and looked around. He could see the Police station across the road and in front was a large Europarking parking garage along Marnixstraat.

The small room consisted of a thin bar with several beer taps. On the other side sat several bar stools, the brick walls were painted black and covered in posters and an ancient looking pockmarked dart board.

An attractive woman looked up at him as he entered, she wore a shirt with a name sewn onto the chest 'Maria', she seemed amused to see him there. 'Halo. Can I help you?' she asked, looking behind him. 'Are you lost?'

James cleared his throat and replied, 'Jared… um, Monsieur Araignée sent me…' the woman instantly lost her smile and squinted her eyes. 'He asked me to give you this and asked if you could help me.' He said holding out the wad of money in his hand.

The woman nodded and walked over to him, took the bundle of money and walked over to the door James had just walked in. She locked the door and then went back to the bar. 'I swear you gangsters are getting younger every day…' Maria lifted a small box from beneath the bar and opened it, throwing the money inside. Maria then walked them through to a shooting range just off the bar area, it was only 4 metres wide and 20 metres long and was split into four small alcoves that housed a shelf to place a gun and ammo. Each alcove had a respective target displayed at the far end of the range. Maria then walked over to a large metal cabinet and unlocked it, sliding the shutters up. Housed inside were dozens of handguns mounted on individual pegs that locked them into position.

Along the sides were hundreds of boxes of ammunition and magazine clips. 'So… Which one first?' she smiled as James walked beside her, his eyes wide and mouth hanging open.

Jared sat in front of Number Two across from her large writing desk. She held a tablet in her hand and swiped from side to side at the photographs displayed upon it. Jared had briefed her on what he had gleaned from the dead Chinese man and now waited for Number Two to process everything.

'We need to know what Chen has in store for us, Jared.' Said Number Two quietly, her eyes scanning each photograph thoroughly. 'Send in your new boy. Chen doesn't know his face and he will be less suspicious.' Jared nodded and stood up.

*

Later that evening James stood in the walk-in wardrobe of Jared's luxury apartment as he turned side to side in front of the full-length mirror. He had put on the new suit Jared had selected for him and it felt good. He turned to see Jared watching him from the door, he hadn't heard him enter.

'Get changed, old hoodie and jeans. You are going undercover.' Spat Jared as he walked back into the kitchen area. James walked in shortly after wearing his old clothes.

Jared explained that he needed James to enter the Westpoort Docks and locate any Chinese persons. He needed photographs, numbers, weapons, vehicles and registration plates. Jared tapped his mobile pulling up a photograph of an angry looking Chinese man in his fifties, sharp suit, styled hair and a small goatee beard and designer glasses.

'This is Chen. Remember this face' Called Jared, 'He has been a pain in Orion's arse before. Chen belongs to one of the most powerful organised-crime families that practically own Hong Kong, Macau and Taiwan.'

'Triads?' asked James, dumbstruck.

'That is correct kiddo, I want you to find him and see what he is up to.'

'You not coming?' asked James cautiously.

'No can-do kiddo… Chen and his boys know my face and I am not exactly inconspicuous.' He laughed pointing at all six foot five of himself. 'Maria told me you had fun today.' Laughed Jared. 'I got you a little something.' He said taking a small thin metal case out from under the worksurface. He laid it down and slid it across to James.

James opened the case to reveal a Jericho 941 automatic pistol developed by the Israeli Military. It was sometimes called the 'Little Desert Eagle' as it was the smaller brother of the infamous Desert Eagle .45 firearm. This pistol took smaller 9×19mm Parabellum rounds, sixteen to be exact. The case housed the pistol, two magazines and a custom silencer.

'And this is for you to take along with you tonight.' Said Jared throwing a silver canister over to James.

'Spray-paint…' said James suspiciously, 'What about this.' He said tapping the gun case.

'Not until you graduate kiddo.' Jared laughed again and placed his large hands on the worktop. 'First jobs start small – building up to… Well to this.' He said tapping the gun case again.

James walked along the Westelijk Havengebied neighbourhood in the centre of Westpoort industrial estate. He hadn't anticipated how large the area was going to be and just how many units there were around Westpoort. He had been walking for two hours, and so far, he hadn't seen anything suspicious and not a single Oriental gentleman. After another hour of walking, he crossed over the main road along from the Zenith Energy Amsterdam Terminal B.V. where James could see a large group of men shouting at one another near the Hitachi Construction Machinery unit. These men didn't sound Dutch, they sounded Chinese.

James crouched down behind a series of crates as he attempted to get a better view of what was going on. He could see a large cargo ship with

'Hanjin Beijing' written along the side was mooring up beside the Zenith Energy terminal, along the ship's gunwale stood dozens of men, some in high-vis safety jackets others in dark coats. James took out his phone and recorded the men as they clambered down off the ship onto the terminal decking. The men shouted at each other then pointed over to where James had taken refuge. He ducked just in time as the majority of them looked directly at him. Moments later a black vehicle pulled up beside the large cargo ship as two men got out of the rear of the vehicle. James risked another look and managed to take a photograph of the vehicle's number plate, then the two men who had just alighted the vehicle. He turned back behind his cover to look at the photographs he had taken. One of the men looked very similar to Chen, but he no longer had a beard, and his hair was much longer. James waited for the men to disperse before he chanced another look, only this time one of the men in the high-vis jackets was staring right at the crates and there was not a chance that he hadn't been spotted. He slipped his phone into his boxer short elastic and grabbed the spray can from his pocket as he hurriedly sprayed something onto the nearest crate.

Seconds later the Chinese man grabbed James by the collar and pulled him up against one of the wooden crates.

'你在做什麼?' spat the man in the high-vis jacket. James quickly translated what he was saying <What are you doing?> This is why he had taken Oriental languages, with over 1.4 billion people speaking the language it was second only to English.

'I am sorry!' shouted James. James intentionally dropped the spray paint canister against the man's feet causing the man to look down. 'Don't tell my parents, please.' Begged James, just as Jared had told him to, *"Play the victim, cry a little and look like you are about to piss your shorts."*

The Chinese man laughed and called over to the others who were making their way over to see who he was and what he was doing. One man in the dark coats joined them picking up the spray paint and shook his head tutting. He slapped James hard across the cheek and laughed. 'Naughty boy.'

The others laughed and one called out in a dialect that James didn't understand. They moved away as the two men returned to their vehicle and drove off back towards the Hitachi building.

'Please…' said James again looking at the two men still holding him.

'讓他走.' Shouted the high-vis man. <Let him go.>

The dark coat man pinched James' cheeks and laughed again. 'Don't come back here.' He punched James in the stomach and stepped back. He called to the high-vis man and they both walked back to the cargo ship where more crates were being craned off. James held his sore stomach and bent to pick up the spray can and looked at the crate he now leant against, winded once again for the countless time that week. He tried the lid, but it was sealed with dozens of long nails. The two men turned back and shouted after him as he ran off.

James sat at Jared's kitchen table and showed him the photographs he had taken.

'Sure looks like him, new hair-do and he's lost some weight… Well done kiddo.' Smiled Jared, flicking through the photographs. 'How is your stomach?' asked Jared, concerned.

James looked over to him, a heavy frown on his face. 'How did you… You were watching me?'

Jared nodded and scoffed. 'You don't think I would let you go unsupervised… Your uncle would have my blerrie head.' He handed the phone back and sat back against the dining chair, his large hand tapping the table. 'We need to know where they are hiding and what they are planning.' Jared looked across to James and smiled trying to lighten the severity of what they were dealing with, 'I will run the number plate of the vehicle to see what comes back. You did good James.' Jared stood up tapping the registration into his own phone as he walked to the fridge. 'You hungry?' He opened the fridge door and scanned the three items inside, he shook his head and turned back to James. 'Let's go out for dinner tonight eh kiddo.' He smiled slamming the empty fridge door.

They walked along Daniël Stalpertstraat until they reached their destination, Restaurant Zaza's was a stylish and very popular establishment. The sleek glossed wood effect tables matched the wall décor that ran the entire length of the restaurant, all illuminated by the elegant down lighting. The two of them settled at the rear of the building away from the entrance. Jared sitting with his back against the wall and James with his back to the other guests. They previewed the menus and ordered some drinks, all seemed typical of two people dining out until Jared's eyes kept flitting to his left towards the other corner of the room. 'What is it?' asked James inquisitively.

'You see those men over there?' asked Jared almost in a whisper, taking the large neatly folded napkin from underneath his cutlery. James turned to see four Chinese men sitting across the room from them. Visibly intoxicated by their language and boisterous and lively behaviour. James nodded and turned back to Jared who scowled at them, his large shoulders seemed to grow as he hunched forward, both his hands concealed beneath their table.

'I am going to slide a napkin towards you which you will take and discreetly hide under your top. You will then walk quickly toward the rest room and wait just inside for me. After I enter you will then leave and ensure that after those four men follow me in, which they will. Nobody else is to come inside.' He stared at James sliding over the now bulky napkin across the shiny wood effect table. 'Do you understand?' he barked. James nodded and took the napkin tucking under his top, he could feel the cold metal of Jared's Beretta 418 against his bruised stomach. Jared stood and walked over to the table as the four Chinese men stopped their loud conversation and turned to ogle at him. He remained silent until one of them stood to confront him, the man wasn't even up to his shoulders but the drink inside him compensated for his short stature. James hurried to the restroom door and glanced once more over his shoulder and Jared was seen whispering something into the ear of the standing man.

James entered the somewhat glamourous restroom and looked around, it consisted of polished concrete, worked wood and chrome with an overkill of down lighting that reflected off of every surface. He checked that all the stalls were free then turned back to the door as Jared walked in, his dark cold eyes moving left to right as he scanned the entire room, he walked to James without looking at him and removed the discreated pistol from James top. Nodding once towards the door James left without another word. Just as Jared had described the four intoxicated Chinese men were walking towards the restroom door. One had a steak knife in his hand, another had taken the large Dutch beer bottle from their table. The two others held their hands inside their jackets, leaving James with only speculation as to what they had hidden away. The bathroom door swung open as the four of them walked inside, James could see Jared with his back to them, his face visible in the mirror above the sink. James recognised that look in his eyes.

James ran to the door and stood there as sentry just as he had been instructed, making sure no one else entered. Inside he heard muffled words of drunken abuse and threats of violence. Then all became silent. He strained his ears to try and ascertain what was transpiring inside then all hell broke loose making him step back from the door.

Jared waited for the door to close; he eyed all four in the mirror as they stood in a line behind him. He checked them one at a time, left to right, inside his head he took notes. *'Left-handed, beer bottle, looks strong… right-handed… shit – big steak knife… right-handed, what is that? Another knife… right-handed, extending baton, Hobbit… Really pissed.'* He turned to face the four of them, his large arms bulging from his tight muscle fit t-shirt as he opened his empty hands. On seeing he was unarmed the four drunk men started their taunts and abuse. The lefty with the bottle walked forward two steps waving the dark green glass at Jared as he shouted. The short man to the far side whipped the extending baton open with a smooth downward flick of the wrist.

Jared stood patiently, silently as the man with the bottle took another step forward raising his left hand. Jared sniffed heavily then lunged forward grabbing the bottle in one hand as his other hand grabbed the man's groin, squeezing *hard*. He lifted him up from the ground several inches causing the man onto tiptoes before smashing the bottle over the startled man's head sending him and the broken green glass to the floor. The man sobbed with both hands grabbing his nether regions as he whimpered in a foetal position. Jared looked across to the little man with the baton as they charged at each other. Ducking he just missed the long metal arm of the baton as it swished over his head; he released a devastating uppercut as he quickly stood upright, sending the little man's head backwards against his neck with a snap dazing him. Jared dodged to his right as a large steak knife jabbed at his chest from his left, the man now right beside them readying himself for another slashing attack. The third man moved in from the right meaning Jared now had nowhere to go. The baton man stood in the middle shook his head as his eyes blurred from Jared's hard punch and too many beers. The man to Jared's right flipped his knife in his hand so the blade pointed downward as he walked forward, his free hand was held out to protect his ribs, head, and neck. *'This guy knows what he is doing...'* thought Jared to himself. The two knife wielding men moved in as one, flanking him as they raised their blades, spinning them in flashes of silver as they mocked slashes and stabs towards him.

Jared waited for them to make their move, and it didn't take them long. First from the right, then the left they released volley after volley at him as he dodged, blocked and parried what he could. Then he found his opening, the professional knife man on the right knocked into his fallen friend causing him to look down for a split second, this was long enough for Jared. With a swift grab, sharp twist and snapping fold of the knife man's wrist he sent him down to his knees with a thud. Followed with a sudden knee to the face the man was out cold. The baton man was back with another wild swing that landed heavily onto the polished concrete wash basin beside Jared. The steak knife came in from the left slashing Jared across the chest as he dived backwards, it was superficial but stung with a vengeance. His hand touched a small glass perfume atomiser beside the sink, he picked it up spraying baton man in the face as he screwed up his eyes in agony dropping the baton into Jared's free hand. One quick swing shot to the side of the man's knee, another to the ribs and he was on the floor scratching at his red eyes. Jared rotated the extending baton in his hand and walked forward as the last man backed off, knife still raised and trained on Jared's large bleeding chest. Jared threw the baton at the man using all of his immense strength making the Chinese man recoil and shield his face as it thumped into his knife hand. As soon as Jared had released the baton, he had sprinted at the last attacker raising his large arm above his shoulder clenching his fist like a hammer as he swung down with a thundering blow into the shielding man's face sending him to the floor unconscious.

Jared stood tall exhaling heavily as he touched the large gash across his heaving chest. *'Dumkop…'* he swore as he turned to check the room. The cool water from the tap was refreshing against his bloodied hands as he washed them in the basin. Red streaks trickled and splattered the pure white porcelain and concrete counter like exploding Morello cherries before the water ran transparent once more. Movement in the large mirror caught his sharp eye as the bottle man had managed to get back up onto his hands and knees and attempted a dashed rugby tackle into Jared's back pushing him hard into the polished concrete block. With a roar Jared turned and punched the attacker hard in the back of the head, sending him sliding down so that he was now wrapped around Jared's ankles. Pulling him up by the hair with one hand Jared tilted the Chinese man's head back, releasing a hard uppercut to the man's chin sending him spread eagled to the tiled floor. Jared shook his hand then bent down so he was beside the semi-conscious man.

'I have some questions for you…' started Jared. His cold eyes fixed on the bottle man. 'We can do this the easy way…' he said, pulling the Beretta from his rear waistband pointing it straight at the man's face, 'Or we can do this the really easy way…'

Three minutes later Jared walked out of the rest room as James stood in a panic, 'What took you so long? They've called the police.' He spat as soon as he saw Jared. 'Come on.'

The two of them walked hastily to the exit as some of the staff followed them outside, their phones pressed to their ears obviously relaying their every step to the police on the other end, another staff member braved to enter the rest room to see what had happened only to run out again screaming holding his mouth as if he was about to vomit.

'It's a blerrie shame…' started Jared as they started jogging away from the scene. 'I really liked that restaurant.' He smiled as they turned a corner. 'And this was my favourite shirt.' He laughed as he looked down at the large blood-stained rip and gash in his muscular chest.

Running beside Jared, James checked over their shoulder, all was clear, so he asked his questions, 'What happened in there?' he said inquisitively.

'A good old-fashioned punch up kiddo.' Spat Jared.

'I can only assume they were Chen's men… But why didn't you just use your gun?' asked James.

'I needed the exercise…' he laughed as they ran down another alleyway. 'Besides, if I shot them all I wouldn't be able to interrogate them.' They arrived at a bustling coffee shop and walked to the back room. The tattooed female at the counter greeted Jared with a knowing smile. Through another door and they were in a small office space, an old cheap peeling wood effect Formica office desk and a stained and gaffa taped swivel chair sat along one wall and several rows of messy overcrowded filing cabinets along the other. Jared pulled his ruined t-shirt off and opened one of the filing cabinet drawers taking out a clean pale-yellow t-shirt and dark blue hoodie. He walked over to the desk and rummaged the drawers until he popped up again with a small first aid box. Cracking it open he threw it on top of the curled edges of the wood effect Formica surface and tore open some steri-wipes before cleaning the drying blood from his chest. Several self-adhesive patches later he had managed to cover the gash. He pulled on the t-shirt only for the pale-yellow to turn a dark colour across his chest as the fresh blood seeped through the bandages.

'You need to see a doctor.' Said the tattooed female from the office door as she watched him slip on the dark hoodie with a wince.

'Later…' spat Jared as he picked up his mobile phone jabbing the screen before holding up to his ear. 'Right now, we have work to do.'

It only took two rings before it was answered. James could hear a female voice on the other end. Jared relayed the previous thirty minutes and the new information he had *acquired* during his visit to the restroom. James sat in silence as he listened to what had happened.

Jared hung up and tapped the phone screen several times as he frowned heavily. Looking up at James he released a half smile. 'Your number plate has come back…' he turned the phone around so James could see the screen. 'Want to test out your new toy?'

James sat in the passenger seat of a huge 4x4 as it raced along the A7 motorway. Jared had his phone wedged between his shoulder and ear as he used both hands to drive and shift gear as they swerved in and out of the evening's traffic. James watched out of the windscreen as they passed the other vehicles as they crossed the 25 km long and very flat Afsluitdijk bridge. Up ahead James read the blue road sign as it flared in their bright head lights beam '1200m Zurich, Harlingen, Leeuwarden'.

Turning off towards the security gated Beach Resort Makkum Jared slowed the engine as he eyed the house numbers and small cul-de-sacs of static caravans, holiday homes and villas. Before he smiled broadly, 'Got ya'

He tapped the steering wheel as they carried on along the road turning off at the next junction parking up behind several stationary vehicles. He climbed out and walked around to James' side and opened his door.

'Take out your pistol.' He barked as he watched James do as he was ordered. 'You only ever use this as a last resort. It is there to protect you… NOT to kill people. I don't want you having to live with the demons that come from taking a life, especially as you are just a blerrie child. You hear me kiddo?' James nodded, attached the silencer and slipped his now loaded Jericho 941 pistol into his shoulder holster before pulling on his raincoat zipping it up to the top.

They walked back past the house where the vehicle he had seen Chen using at Westpoort was parked up. The sleek black vehicle was a beautiful, customised brand-new Mercedes. The property looked nice, pristine patios and manicured gardens surrounded by a low hedge and tall wall for privacy meaning it was not possible to see who or what was inside from the road.

'Jared...' started James as he looked around. 'This doesn't feel right.' He looked around him at the other neighbouring properties full of happy families on vacation, people carriers and saloons parked up on driveways with trunks piled high with luggage, child seats and bike racks. Not the area you would expect to see the head of a major crime family hiding out.

Jared nodded but looked back over to the vehicle parked outside of the rental home.

'Go and knock on the door, ask if Jasper is home and if he can come out to play.' Spat Jared handing him some AirPod earphones. 'Put these in your ears and act dumb.'

'I'm not a ten-year-old!' protested James. 'That won't work.'

'Trust me.' Replied Jared as he ducked back behind the wall pushing James towards the small gate.

James did as he was told and put the headphones in and marched over to the rental property's front door. He knocked loud and stepped back waiting in anticipation as to who would open the door. To his surprise a young attractive Indian woman answered the door. 'Can I help you?' she asked with an honest smile. James nodded and asked if Jasper was home to which the young woman looked lost.

'He told me to call on him to ask if he could come and play.' Said James pointing over his shoulder with his thumb.

'No sorry, maybe try one of the neighbours.' She replied sincerely as she went to close the door on him. James felt like an idiot, they had the wrong house, or Jared had bad intelligence on the vehicle. Most likely using false plates. Behind her a male voice could be heard. James listened as the young woman explained the situation but as the door was about to close a hand pulled it back open. Standing in the doorway was the Chinese driver who had been standing next to Chen. James was certain it was him, the one from the photograph on his phone. The man came outside walking right up to James, then looked all around the street and garden. 'What you want?' spat the man indignantly. 'Who are you?'

'I am looking for Jasper…' started James awkwardly, 'He gave me this address.' The Chinese man didn't seem so happy as he continued forward causing James to walk backwards and out towards the gate.

'Wrong house… You go now.' Spat the Chinese man aggressively, shooing James away with his hand. James turned and jogged away down the road until he was out of sight of the angry man. James stood as his hands and legs began to shake again. He focused on his breathing, slow inhale, long exhale, repeat. He started feeling better when a large hand suddenly pulled him back into the hedge row causing him to scream through the hand over his mouth, he turned trying to unzip his raincoat to free his pistol as he saw Jared's large face shushing him with a finger over his lips.

'Did you see?' started James in excitement as Jared let him go.

'Yes, it was the chauffeur.' Replied Jared dryly. 'No sign of Chen though.' He tutted in annoyance. 'Might have to go fishing.'

James watched the LED clock in the 4x4 dash flick to 02:00 AM as the vehicle door opened making him jump, Jared's face appeared with a squint eye and bloodied nose. 'Give me a blerrie hand.' He said as he walked towards the back of the vehicle dragging something heavy behind him. James jumped out running around to help him when he realised Jared was pulling a black heavy duty PVC mortuary body bag along the floor. James' eyes opened wide. But Jared just laughed at him. 'He is just unconscious.'

James opened the boot, the benefit of such a large 4x4 was the excessive boot space which easily accommodated an unconscious six-foot Chinese man restrained in a coroner's body bag. Jared exhaled as he climbed into the driver's seat and delicately touched his tender nose. 'Son-of-a-bitch was tough.' He spat as he started the engine. 'But not tough enough.'

James decided not to ask Jared about the midnight home invasion or where he had learnt such techniques. But it had worked and they had their bait.

Pulling away they made their way back to the long Afsluitdijk bridge. The road was almost deserted by all other vehicles, with only two headlights far off behind them in the distance. The darkness on either side of the bridge made the journey feel eerie to James. He was not only tired but a little on edge about the whole 'abduction' scenario. He watched as the silently desolate petrol station in the middle of the bridge came into view ahead of them. He thought it an odd location for a service station, slap bang in the middle of a huge bridge. He watched it pass then looked in the wing mirror as they continued along the empty road. This was when he noticed the headlights behind them. Somewhat closer than when they had entered the bridge. 'Jared…' he started, anxiety filling his stomach as he sat up straight.

'I see them kiddo.' Spat the large man next to him. They lurched back into their seats as Jared revved the four-litre engine. His foot flat to the ground.

Chapter 7

The Big Plan

Afsluitdijk Bridge, A7 Motorway, North of Amsterdam.

Jared was already going at 190 kmph as the 4x4 raced along the empty motorway. The two vehicles behind them relentlessly gained on them through the darkness. He held his phone to his ear as he cursed to himself, *'Dumkop'*

'We have contact, two vehicles are in pursuit.' He spat into the phone. 'Weapons not known but likely.' The rear window exploded inwards as he spoke causing him to swerve as he struggled to regain control of the speeding vehicle. 'Weapons are hot, we are taking fire. Requesting air support.'

With the rear windscreen now gone James could hear multiple cracking pop sounds from behind them. He looked in the wing mirror to see intermittent orange flashes emitting either side of the two vehicles as their pursuing occupants continued to discharge their firearms at them. James pulled out his Jericho 941 and turned in his seat. Jared looked across at him, his face visibly torn between not wanting the young man to lose his innocence but also knowing that he couldn't drive and effectively return fire at their pursuers. He nodded and James began returning fire. The Jericho had been his preferred weapon during his visit with Maria. The elegant look, satisfying feel and effective firepower of the pistol made it his choice of firearm. But he soon discovered shooting a speeding vehicle in the dark was very different to shooting a well-lit stationary target from 20 metres away.

He knelt in the passenger seat facing backwards, one arm either side of the head rest. The pistol in his right hand, his left underneath in a supportive hold. He took aim with each shot, the adrenaline rushing his body as he fought to keep his shaking hands steady. He looked up suddenly as the gun stopped firing, the chamber was stuck back revealing the front inch of the barrel, he was now only emitting empty clicks when he squeezed the trigger. 'Reload!' he shouted to himself as he released the magazine and slipped in another before re-chambering the barrel. Sixteen shots left.

The two vehicles were now only metres away from them as they continued along the empty bridge. Jared continued to bark down his phone as James continued to shoot at the – James stopped. The lead pursuing vehicle suddenly swerved erratically to the side colliding with the concrete and steel barrier as the front bumper and wing caved in as it rolled violently 180 degrees through the air and into the dark green murky featureless waters of the ocean below. The remaining vehicle's occupants looked at each other as James continued to fire on them, their windscreen a spider's web of splintered glass. Jared gave a half gaze at James as he continued to focus on the road ahead. James slowed his breathing, took his time knowing he only had several shots left, and aimed for the driver. 'thut, thut, thut.' He was out of ammunition. He turned back in his seat and held the gun up to Jared. 'Empty.' He hollered over the engine as the vehicle behind them bumped into them at just over 200 kmph forcing them both forwards in their seats. James turned to look as the vehicle then slowed and drifted to the central reservation, sparks flying up as it juddered and grinded to an uncooperative stop. The driver either incapacitated or dead. The passenger climbed out and continued to fire but their vehicle was now too far away to cause any significant damage.

Jared nodded to James and squeezed his shoulder encouragingly. Back on his phone he seemed to relax, 'Contact terminated, vehicles are no longer in pursuit.' He slowed as he reached the toll gates on the western end of the bridge. 'Cover your face, James.' He barked pointing to the several ANPR (Automatic Number Plate Recognition cameras) and CCTV ahead of them as his little yellow 'Telepass' prepaid toll reader box in the windscreen beeped loudly. Seconds later the red and white security barrier raised open just in time to allow their vehicle through. 'We will bring the package to the Bravo Charlie.'

"Air support inbound – will escort." came a voice through the handset.

'Understood.' Jared tapped the phone and threw it into the giant array of holders in the centre of the vehicle where the gear stick and handbrake were housed. Overhead the thundering sound of a large military helicopter made them both look up. A sleek Boeing AH-64 Apache roared above them at one hundred feet. 'Late but still appreciated.' Laughed Jared.

Jared slowed as he approached the main city centre of Amsterdam, the roads were clear, and they both felt a little easier knowing their air escort overhead was watching their backs. Jared parked up at an industrial estate on the outskirts and waited as two non-descript trader transit vans pulled up alongside them. He gave a nod and alighted the vehicle picking up his phone. Several people filed out of the transit vans and began removing their cargo from the large 4x4's boot, lifting the man into one of the vans before it drove off. Jared and James walked over as several people from the other van took their keys and drove off with the smashed up giant 4x4. The helicopter drifted off towards the airport as James looked around them, now completely deserted and alone in the middle of a desolate industrial estate at three in the morning. 'So now what?' he asked before he suddenly vomited all over his shoes.

The next morning James woke to find himself in the spare room of Jared's Warehouse apartment. He checked his phone to see what time it was and juddered as he stretched out the sleep in his limbs. He could hear music and clattering from the kitchen, a beautiful aroma of coffee and the sweet breads that European breakfasts are famous for. He clambered out of bed rubbing his tired eyes.

'Good morning boss.' He said as he sat down at the breakfast bar.

Jared looked at him in silence, then eased a smile out. 'Your uncle Max would be proud of you. You really came through last night. You are a credit to both your father and Max.' he threw a small package over to James as he turned back to the frying pan turning over the thick cut bacon. 'If it ain't smoked, it ain't bacon.' He smiled to himself taking a big whiff through his bruised nose.

James unwrapped the package to find a new mobile phone, a generic bank card, a wedge of what looked like €2000 in crisp banknotes and two new loaded magazine cartridges for his pistol. He looked up to Jared with a lost expression.

'What are these for?' he asked inquisitively, turning the phone on.

'A pat on the back from Number Two...' replied Jared nonchalantly. He casually fished the bacon out of the pan with his spatula placing it gracefully onto the two plates beside him. 'Today you graduate, kiddo.' Said Jared seriously, his cold dark eyes making James shudder. 'Congratulations.'

*

'You have not asked what we do here at Orion.' Smiled Number Two as she sipped her large black coffee. James didn't answer so she answered for him. 'We work towards a better future for mankind.' She lay back on the chair and tapped one of the remotes causing one of the large screens across from them to blink into life showing an old BBC News broadcast of Manchester, England from several years back.

She read off what was displayed on the screen, '22 May 2017 Manchester Arena bombing kills 22. Local terrorist cell. On the 5th July 2005 a splinter cell was challenged by the UK government. So, on 7th July they pushed back - London Bus Bombing - 52 UK residents of 18 different nationalities were killed and more than 700 were injured in the attacks.' She tapped as each one was displayed on the large screen. She put her coffee cup down and continued, another tap, another news story broadcast. 'Going further back, the Lockerbie Bombing 21st December 1988, flight 103 Pan Am 259 deaths.' She turned to James and blinked several times. 'What does Orion do Mr Bond?'

James thought for a moment then answered. 'These are all terrorist attacks. Orion must be one of two states... First thought is that you are an anti-terrorism organisation. Or secondly...' he looked her in the eye as he said this. 'You support terrorism.'

Number Two scoffed and picked up her coffee and she tapped another button, 'We were not responsible for any of these atrocities... The only way we could be held remotely responsible is that we failed to stop them in time… 17th December 1983, car bomb outside of Harrods store, Hans Crescent, London 6 deaths.' She sipped silently, 'London knew about this, as did the CIA… But they sat back and watched. Do you have any idea why?' she asked rhetorically, answering before he could reply. 'Because terror keeps people in fear, making them easily controlled and more bias to vote in favour of extreme solutions.'

'Do you think the people of America and England would have agreed so freely to go to war in the Middle East in 2001 if the atrocities at the World Trade Centre hadn't happened?'

James watched her as she spoke, she had a professional manner but her passion was genuine. This was no act or role play. Number Two was unwaveringly committed and devoted to their cause.

She swirled her coffee in the cup before taking another swig, licking her lips. 'Governments procrastinate, dawdle. Hide behind red tape and bureaucracy. Whereas at Orion, we take action, we fight back and we proactively problem solve.'

James raised an eyebrow but remained silent. Number Two stood up and walked around to stand beside him. 'The world is full of very bad people, Mr Bond. We target those that are the most risk to society. Orion restores the balance of the actions of such people. We act when governments fail.'

'So, you're vigilantes?' asked James.

'We are liberators… Saviours.' She retorted resolutely and dutifully firm. 'We fight back where others simply hide or plead ignorance.'

'Do you act as pariahs… Or do you have backing from world governments?' he asked earnestly.

Number Two walked back to her desk, 'We have funding from world governments… But backing?' she shook her head with a tired smile. 'That is debatable. Politics is a game played by fools who believe they have power. We have no interest in politics or children's squabbles. We act when the governments fail. Orion sets out to heal and rescue the world from the depravity that it is sinking into.' She stopped and clicked another screen as tables and statistics appeared on it. 'Crime rates continue to increase year on year, prisons occupancy quadruples every ten years until there is no space, so more prisons need to be built or the Crown Prosection Service releases well behaved murderers and rapists back into society because they have nowhere else to put them. Desperate Police forces performances worsen under the crippling cutbacks year on year from their respective governments, the inexplicable load of corruption and fatigue breaking the proverbial camel's back, coupled by the growing trend and popularity for vicious crime, gang culture and unhealthy debauchery of a sick humankind.' She tapped again as a large pie chart appeared on the second screen, 'Just look at the number of re-offenders that have been failed by the world's criminal justice systems…' she huffed indignantly.

'You plan to rehabilitate them?' James laughed softly, shaking his head.

'No Mr Bond…' started Number Two. 'We endeavour to *remove* them from society,' she smiled psychotically, 'It is proven time and time again that the current system does not work. If the relenting rate of crime continues like this, within 34 years the police forces of Europe will crumble and be forced to disband, and the prison systems will be overrun and made redundant.' She walked back to the first screen that now flicked through the dozens of terrorist attacks. '84% of the offenders responsible for the atrocities you see here were "Under observation" by MI5, MI6, CIA, EU and Interpol Counter Terrorism and The Hague. Yet none of these organisations managed to stop these vile attacks.' She tapped another button as multiple photographs and videos appeared showing nefarious looking men and woman all over the world, some appeared to be war lords in African states, some tribesman from Afghanistan in remote caves, others posting anonymous videos from bedrooms with backdrops of radical flags and antisemitic iconography. 'These, James…' she pointed at the photographs and videos on the screen, 'These we did manage to stop. Orion has saved millions of lives by working in the shadows and taking action when it is most needed. Sometimes with the permission, support and backing of world governments, sometimes not.' She shrugged indifferently.

'So, you terrorise the terrorists?' he asked.

'Orion has spent years infiltrating the criminal world, both visibly, politically and surreptitiously. Our ideology is to strike the very heart and remove crime from the world in one swift move.' Number Two's eyes glared with vigour and excitement as she spoke. James watched her very carefully.

'And how may I ask, do you plan to carry out this Herculean undertaking?' asked James.

'Project Tabula Rasa.' She glowed matter of factly.

'Tabula Rasa? As in a blank slate?' questioned James.

Number Two placed a hand on the table as she leant in closer to James, 'Orion will cleanse the world, re-educate the world and rebuild the world.' Her eyes grew wide with passion.

'Orion operates 72% of all the illegal drugs moving in and out of mainland Europe.' Number Two started as she once again sat at her desk. 'Orion has agents in every human trafficking ring, sex trade and child abduction rings in every major country of the world.'

'Sounds extremely profitable.' Remarked James uncomfortably.

'Dangerous… Mr Bond, it is extremely dangerous. As successful and careful as we are, other organisations such as Chen's Triads attempt to move in and eliminate our organisation, putting everything at risk. We are at our zenith and almost ready to severe the head of organised crime.' She smiled eagerly.

James was intrigued but ultimately scared by her devotedness and pure sociopathic ideology. 'Severing the head?' He asked openly.

'When you are the only baker in the village, everyone eats your bread.' she replied.

James looked at her, unsure of the German Analogy.

'If the bread is tainted, everyone in the village dies.' she continued.

James nodded, finally understanding their approach. 'So you plan to intentionally poison 75% of Europe's drug supply, then clean up what's left?'

'Very good Mr Bond, I am impressed.' Number Two smiled. 'That is the first phase of Project Tabula Rasa.'

'That ideology must make you an awful lot of enemies?' retorted James. 'Both externally and internally. What if someone doesn't want you to sever the head... If you stop crime, you stop your income. Have you thought about that?' he questioned openly.

The door behind them opened as *Number One* entered the room. Number Two stood and bowed as she walked towards James ushering him up from his seat. *Number One* sat on the lip of the large desk and called over to James. 'It would seem you have proven yourself to Orion Mr Bond. I have just watched your courageous act on the Afsluitdijk Bridge last night. This pleases me.'

Number Two walked James to the door as she whispered, 'We are approaching the final stage of our operation, we will call you when you are next needed.' As the German woman ushered him out of the door James could hear other voices from within the room, emitting from the speakers built into the long conference table. James heard them mentioning the Chinese driver that he had helped bring in earlier that morning.

'*Wei Lin Lee has disclosed Chen's location and proposed plan of attack.*' Said one of the bodiless voices.

'Irrelevant!' snapped *Number One* belligerently. 'Seeing as Chen undoubtedly knows we have him, that location and plan are now obsolete.' The door closed with a vacuum seal, and all became silent.

Jared was waiting for James outside the building, and he was glad for the familiar company. 'What are your thoughts on Number Two?' asked James openly as they walked to the crossing.

'She's too old for you kiddo.' Laughed Jared in response.

'No… I mean-' started James frustratedly.

'I know what you meant.' Spat Jared. He took out his phone and held his finger over his lips shaking his head. 'Let's grab some lunch and we can have a chat.' He tapped his ear then the phone to suggest that Orion was listening to their conversation.

Walking to the Café het Paleis along Paleisstraat just west of the Royal Palace Amsterdam they ordered some food to go and sat outside in the warm mid-afternoon sunshine opposite the cafe at a bench overlooking the quiet canal. The bridges roads and footpaths were unnaturally quiet due to a series of bright traffic cones cordoning off abandoned road works and the adjacent car park had been suspended meaning they had the area to themselves. Jared took one of the café's paper napkins adorned with the establishment's crown logo and popped a pen into his mouth biting off the lid he scribbled something down and showed it to James who was eating his sandwich. *"Talk normally, they will know if you act suspicious."* His eyebrow raised.

'So…' started Jared, nodding, screwing up the napkin, 'You want to know about Number Two?'

'Honestly… I want to know about all of them.' Started James looking around. 'The whole concept seems a little unbelievable…' He tore a bite of his sandwich and chewed angrily. 'Is she for real?' he asked earnestly.

'Oh, she is real alright kiddo.' Laughed Jared. 'She has worked her way up over many years, and now she is answerable only to *Number One.*' He slurped on his drink and wiped his bruised face with a paper napkin. 'She is crazily adherent… And dangerous with it. None of us know her full back story, but I did hear that she worked as an Inspector for the BPOL, Bundespolizei or German federal police. She was successful, a career of over ten years then… Something happened. The trauma behind her drastic reasoning or agenda has not been disclosed to us mere minions but something happened to her and now she despises the evils of this world.'

'What about Orion?' asked James cautiously. 'Their views are equally extremist and radical. They are talking about actual genocide.' Said James seriously putting down his food, his appetite dwindling. 'Have you not had your doubts about their motives?'

'Motives?' repeated Jared.

'They are talking about purging thousands of people for the purpose of stopping crime. How hypocritical is that?' he scoffed somewhat bewildered.

'You sound so naïve James.' Spat Jared. 'You any idea how many of the world's governments are responsible for thousands of deaths every year. What do you think they do? What your MI5 and MI6 actually do?' Jared turned to look James in the eye. 'The powers that be, be they British, American, FSB, Israeli, Chinese or whoever else decides to stand up and play God. Choices are made every day who shall live and who shall die without hesitation.' He clicked his fingers as he spoke. 'The ethos has always been *"Kill one to save a thousand."* But they never disclose how many *one* actually is.'

'Do you believe they will actually sever the head of organised crime?' asked James disbelievingly.

'Many countries have attempted it, and many have come close. But the problem is an ancient one, much like The Lernaean Hydra. You cut one head off and two more grow back. China came the closest, in that they arrested all known drug dealers and drug users and publicly executed them. Using this as a visual deterrent, it worked for a few weeks, but then the Chinese authorities realised that even with the risk of being beheaded people still wanted their dirty fix. And within a single month drugs were being distributed back into the streets. It is like trying to stop a tidal flood with a bucket.'

'There is too much at risk here Jared, too much power and money to just have it stop.' Quibbled James. 'Do they really believe they can pull a plug on this and expect it to go smoothly?'

'That is not for us to concern ourselves with. We are simply here to push the button when asked.' Replied Jared coldly. 'Like Pawn's on a chess board. The world always needs people like us, James.'

James sat in thought for a few minutes before he looked up and spoke, 'I don't know if I can do this...' Jared looked at him with a concerned raised eyebrow. 'Do you think I am capable of murder?'

Jared sighed heavily then squeezed James shoulder, 'Criminal underworld James... What did you expect? Your uncle Max and I don't want you involved in any of this, but you are implicated now, and you know there is no way out.' James rubbed his head as he tried to process everything.

'Besides,' started Jared with a forced smile. He was trying his best to keep the dire situation positive. 'I see something in your eyes James. That same look your father and uncle had. If you are willing to follow an order that you know deep down will save hundreds of thousands of people, you will do it.' Jared stood and threw his sandwich crust into the canal as several small birds began squabbling over it below them. He turned back to James with a smile, 'You have the bearings of a great soldier James, loyalty, bravery, intelligence and above all else, compassion. That is what will make you stand out from the others. Sure, we are cold ruthless bastards, but sometimes we need soldiers who think before they act, and sometimes we need morality and a blerrie conscience.' Jared's mobile beeped distracting him for a moment, he nodded and called to James. 'We need to get back, come on lets-.' He paused as he watched two men across the road acting suspiciously, they were talking to a young woman dressed as a nun. 'You see that, the blerrie cheek of it.' He spat as he approached them, 'Come on James.'

James shuffled behind him as they approached the nun. Jared stood there silently, arms folded and his face in professional resting bitch mode. The two men stopped talking and walked away quickly keeping their heads down. James stepped forward openly, 'Are you ok?' he asked sincerely. The nun nodded coyly then smiled, her eyes avoiding Jared's all the while.

'That is a bad habit you've got there sister…' sneered Jared. James watched as the nun finally looked at him sucking her teeth with her tongue. 'I thought I told you last time that we don't appreciate your *trouble* on our streets.'

'Neuken!' spat the nun to James' horror. 'Give me a break Spider. I've got to make a living too, you know.'

'James, help this *poes* with her pockets will you.' Ordered Jared still folding his large arms as he watched the little nun. 'Oh, and be careful, she's got a purple belt in Brazilian Jiu Jitsu and every type of Hepatitis you could imagine.' He laughed as she stuck her middle finger up at him.

'Am I missing something here?' asked James uneasily as he turned back to Jared.

'This dummkopf is Estella Mears, dealer, hustler and whore extraordinaire.' Said Jared. 'She has been warned before about dealing on our streets. I fear she may need some encouragement and a gentle reminder that she needs to Voetsak.' Jared leaned in close and whispered into her ear. Her face fell as she looked from James back to Jared. She stuttered timorously and ran off, throwing her black and white veil and bandeau into the canal.

*

James and Jared sat along the long conference table and looked at the paperwork in front of them. James could see several others sitting opposite them. Some were the ones he had fought against during his unorthodox induction. Some ignored him whilst others blatantly glared at him, obviously not very happy with how a teenager had bested them. He saw the young lady with several stitches atop dark bruises to both her lips; she resembled someone who had undergone a cleft palate operation.

Number Two tapped her console as the screens around them came alive. She called out across the vast meeting room as she walked the length of the table. 'Ladies and gentlemen, eyes front… Project Tabula Rasa is in commencement. We begin with phase one, Cleansing.' They all stopped staring and turned to the main screen as one.

'Step one - Operation Free-Bird: The British government's agency G4S Global security services company operate and manage the majority of London's prisons system. On Friday morning at 0800 hours of this week the prisoners under their care will intentionally be let loose to run havoc on the streets of London. Whilst the Metropolitan Police Force are trying to locate all of the escaped convicts, we will initiate Step two - Operation Botox.' She smiled as she double tapped her small computer pad, her eyes fixed to the main screen, projecting her genocidal PowerPoint presentation. 'Operation Botox as previously discussed, but for those who were absent.' she turned to James, 'Orion will infiltrate sixteen water plants across southern UK Mainland. Next Thursday evening we will be releasing concentrated doses of Botulinum toxin into the Thames Water supply, thus contaminating 38% of the United Kingdom's fresh water supply within two hours. Before they know what happened 100% of London's prison population along with 80% of those residents of targeted high crime rate areas will have their life extinct. We will then release the pre-recorded apology message from the Prime Minister and ensure all media coverage and social media trends relate to the unforeseen yet fatal significant contamination found within the processing plants.' She paused and looked around the room, 'Any questions?' She hissed, her eyes mimicking an eagle's watching its prey from across the room. The entire table remained silent.

'In just under three hours' time we will send two teams to England via helicopter from Schiphol to initiate the trial run on the open prison designated "Open Cage", full details are in your dossiers. Our operatives within the prison know not to touch the water, at midnight they will report a gas leak within the compound but by the time it is fully investigated it will transpire to have been a fatal leak. The trial is to confirm the full potency of the toxin before Thursday, our target is for full capacity fatality.' She lowered her tablet and stood at the head of the table, her eyes once again scanning the table. 'Team one,' she started as she pointed her bony finger at Jared, James and a large man sat to their left. 'Bruce, Bond and Maekin.' She turned to point at the other side of the table, 'Team two...' again she pointed at the three sat opposite, 'Jens, Van Der Got and Mino.' She looked at the bruised female sitting beside team two and told her rather than asking, 'Rugen, we will ask you to stay here, your face will cause too many questions and make you too recognisable.' To which the female nodded then glared back across the table at James. Her eyes wide, cold and menacing, making James swallow hard.

Their helicopter was a custom built 8-seater matt black HX50 Luxury Private Helicopter with dark tinted windows and virtually no markings or livery, the front windscreen was a single curved piece of sharply angled impact resistant bullet-proof glass. James was amazed how their van was able to just pull onto the Schiphol runway without stopping for security or customs as it drove right up to their waiting helicopter. It transpired that they were to be piloted by their colleague Mino, James had only just met her that morning, but she was unforgettable. She was a six-foot muscular blonde with the square jawed physique and temperament of a sadistic pro wrestler. She sneered at James and licked her lips as he walked past her climbing into the rear of the luxury chopper. She appeared as if she wanted to eat him whole. Jared laughed, pushing her back gently with a raised eyebrow, commenting to James once they had taken their seat that she was the partner of Rugen, the injured female James had hit with his belt. Mino was just indignant that she couldn't undertake the mission with her girlfriend.

The flight was extremely smooth, short and direct, landing at Biggin Hill Airport, London only an hour later. James saw the rusting relics of the Spitfire and Hurricane planes standing sentinel outside the compound gates as they descended to land. James thought back to what Jared and his uncle Max had told him about their missions in and out of this very airport over the past thirty years. He looked across to Jared who seemed blasé by the entire situation, obviously no nostalgia was held as they touched down.

They stayed inside the helicopter as Mino climbed down to speak to an old man in an oil-stained orange high-vis jacket who approached them. He took one look at Mino and nodded silently, waving over to a people carrier parked near the entrance. It rolled up beside the chopper as they all alighted and climbed in picking Mino up moments later.

The sky flashed above them as a clap of thunder could be heard over the vehicles radio. Rain started tapping against the windscreen and side windows as they drove away into the evening. Their driver pulled up into a layby that had been coned off. Minutes later they were silently transferred into two separate Thames Water maintenance vehicles that had been stowed in the closed layby. James noticed that his team got lumbered with the older dirtier van but decided it best not to mention it to either Jared or Maekin.

The vans wipers squeaked as they shot incessantly across the chipped windscreen trying to clear away the torrent of rain from the grey skies above. James looked out through the driving rain to a small track that led away from the main carriageway to an isolated red brick structure surrounded by a low-level six-foot security fence topped with a thin wisp of barbed wire. Their van rolled to a stop as Maekin, their designated driver, slipped on his baseball cap, turning his stained hi-vis coats collar up around his cauliflowered and scarred ears. He muttered in his native tongue as he opened the van door. His large frame made the vans suspension bounce as he climbed out into the downpour. His round shoulders hunching as he waddled indignantly towards the security gate. Moments later he was wrestling the gate open before he slunk back to the driver's door. He slouched in his seat and blew heavily out of his mouth causing his stubble covered cheeks to wobble.

'Next time you open gate.' He said bitterly in his broken English wiping rain from his face.

He forced the van into gear with a crunch and rolled inside the small compound, stopping next to a large blue door that led into the main structure. Maekin turned and glared at James as he spoke,

'Keep your head down and hood up, avoid CCTV.' He said pointing up at the cheap surveillance that was mounted on the red bricked building in front of them. 'Gloves?' he grunted as all three of them pulled on black nitrile gloves. Maekin approached the security door with a small Kronos Lock Pick Gun, it looked like a miniature Lightsaber but silently opened the door in seconds.

Inside they moved quickly down a narrow corridor that opened into a vast room, a large sign hung from thin wire clips from the stained ceiling tiles above the door, it read: 'PUMP ROOM'. The room consisted of a central raised catwalk that stood easily eight feet off the lowered ground beneath. A single set of metal steps descended into the pump room below. Huge blue pipes with large globe valves emerged from the concrete floor and ran off into the walls on the far end of the room. Above the steps sat an electrical panel covered in a grubby plastic sleeve. The panel was decorated with pressure gauges and dial displays for the technicians to audit and record and ensure all worked appropriately. James walked over to one of the massive pipes and touched its cold surface. He looked at the nearest valve taking note of the large letters embossed on the wheel 'CLOSE' along with a thin arrow either side of it.

"Idiot proof." He said to himself as he readied himself. A hand at either side of the large wheel atop the valve. He looked back to Jared and Maekin and nodded. He spun the wheel down the stem as it became tighter with each rotation. He could hear the pressure building in the large pipe beneath him as the internal plug blocked the flow of the water as the small electrical panel above started beeping irritably.

Jared opened his briefcase and carefully removed three small vials before picking up a large eighteen-inch monkey wrench stowed by the metal steps. He handed it to their disgruntled driver Maekin who speedily removed the seven heavy duty bolts securing the service hatch to the large blue pipes body. He left one bolt attached, the eighth one still in place, allowing the cap to pivot around to expose the inside of the water pipe. Jared then placed one of the vials above the opening and twisted the top off the vial as it released a small hiss, the pressurised contents relieving itself before it was swallowed by the residual water within the bottom of the water pipe. James fought back the sickening rip within his stomach, he inhaled deeply to quieten the outcry building within him. He swallowed hard and let Jared continue without protest. 'The mission comes first kiddo. Government's change, their lies stay the same. We are the change the world needs.' whispered Jared on seeing James' ashen face as he emptied the last two vials and then nodded to Maekin as he hastily replaced the seven bolts.

With a nod and a grin Jared walked back up the steps and tapped several buttons on the control panel, but the beeping still droned on. Jared called out to James to open the valve again which he did. The fizz from within the pipe turned into a roar as the beeping panel suddenly stopped. All returned to normal as they stood there, listening to the muffled water once again rushing through the pipes.

Three minutes later they were back in the van as Maekin was securing the padlock to the security gate. Jared took out his mobile telephone and sent a brief text before revealing a broad smile.

'Mission complete.'

*

James woke with a start as the HX50 helicopter dropped horizontally into Schiphol airport. He felt physically sick, his stomach was full of giant knots that made his guilt feel even stronger. *"They are all criminals."* He kept telling himself as he thought about what they had just done. He kept hearing Jared's voice repeating inside his head, *"They are all nonces, paedophiles and molesters, they deserve everything that is coming for them. The mission comes first."* But James still felt terrible. He had just aided in and condoned the death of hundreds of people.

The drive back to Jared's was a blur.

James stood silently hunched against the shower tiles almost comatose as the hot water hit him in the face, although he felt nothing… He was utterly numb. Jared banged around in the apartment's kitchen as he made them something to eat, which normally consisted of noodles and some chopped vegetables. James felt cold inside, as though he was dreaming and stuck in a state of terror. He tried making himself sick, but nothing came up. He tried crying but nothing came out. He was relying on his inner strength, but it was failing him. He stood in a half daze as he turned off the water. Jared was calling him, their meal ready and waiting for him. James threw on a towel and walked back into his room. He dried himself and dressed almost entirely by muscle memory as his mind replayed what he had just done. "*Why didn't I stop them?*" he repeated. "*Why did I allow them to-*" A series of loud bangs on his door woke him from his inner monologue as he called out to Jared.

'Best not be tossing off on my sheets!' Jared boomed out from the other side of the bedroom door. 'Blerrie dinners getting cold. Come on eh, while it is still lekker.'

James inhaled deeply then opened the door, Jared stood smiling. With a nod he walked off to the kitchen table where two bowls of noodles and fried vegetables sat. James sat down and pulled it towards him playing with it with his cutlery.

'I guess you're struggling with your inner demons kiddo?' said Jared as he devoured a large fork full of noodles. 'Now are the days that you start to feel alive, Live today… Die tomorrow. The darkness will soon pass, you kinda get used to the awful feeling that is ripping your stomach up inside. Evil is no more, and victory is ours.' He nodded with a grin to the large flat screen television on the wall. It was muted but displayed the news broadcast, live with an aerial view of a decrepit prison in England. James swallowed hard and tried to look away, but he couldn't. His eyes scanned the bottom of the screen to try and take in all the details as words rolled across.

'How many died?' he asked through a dry mouth.

Jared sniffed and laughed hard, 'None!' he shook his head incredulously. 'Turns out this was just another blerrie test of loyalty. Those three vials contained nothing more than tap water. This is just a report about an old con who passed away from old age. One of the Great Train robbery suspects from the 60's.' He laughed unmuting the television as a black and white mug shot photograph appeared of a bruised man with slicked hair standing before the uniformed rows of a height chart. 'We were sent on a fool's errand kiddo.' Slurped Jared through another mouthful.

'I don't understand…' James started. 'Why send six people in a helicopter, risking getting caught on the false pretence that we were going to murder all of those people?' He spat angrily, dropping his fork into the noodle bowl. 'What the actual f-' shouted James irritably, cutting himself off as Jared stood suddenly.

'Looks like there is a mole within the Amsterdam office of Orion,' answered Jared sternly. 'And *Number One* wanted to test our two teams.'

'A mole?' repeated James. 'They think it is me?' he asked, now very scared.

'If they did, we wouldn't be sitting here having dinner kiddo. We would be laying on the floor, hog tied with several bullets in the back of our heads.' Jared slurped another large fork of noodles, licking his lips. 'Someone has been passing information onto Chen.'

*

Chapter 8

The Rise

Rijksmuseum, Amsterdam.

James and Jared walked through the busy streets towards the 19th century façade of the Rijksmuseum, both in utter silence. Jared's face displayed his downright frustration and confusion from the morning's escapades whilst James blew out his cheeks for the hundredth time since leaving the apartment, the nausea fading but he still felt weak and drained from exhaustion.

The museum was rammed with thousands of visitors, tourists, art students and school trips milling around admiring all the masterpieces of the Dutch Golden Age. James struggled to keep up with Jared's determined strides as they picked their way through the thronged mass of people into a room filled with models of ships, vessels and tugs, the vaulted ceilings tickled by the hundreds of masts and sails illuminated by the many blinding spotlights above the display cabinets.

Jared stopped beside a grand looking galleon ship atop a small black plinth. The models rigging stood at over twenty feet tall with all sails out on display, two rows of miniature cannon protruded out of the bulging gunwales and the bows gilded decoration gleamed in the museum's canopy of halogen bulbs glory. Beside them stood a young black man in a polo shirt and khaki shorts, an Audio-Tour device clamped to his ear as he took photographs with the mobile phone in his spare hand. He lowered his phone but kept the audio device held high as he started talking to himself almost in a whisper. His eyes looked forward the entire time, moving up and down the towering masts of the galleon ship. James could just make out what he was saying over the hundreds of people that filed past them.

'Word is that Chen has arranged a meet with someone from Orion this afternoon.' The unknown man paused as he typed in another number into his Audio-Tour device before replacing it back to his ear. 'A large shipment came in from the east that will disrupt Orion's output, whoever it is that is meeting Chen has made an offer to *assist* in the distribution of Chen's product… As an act of peace.'

James could see Jared's eye flare as he muttered a profanity under his breath. 'Where?' asked Jared as he leant in close to the Galleon as if to admire the fine decoration of the gilding timber and rigging.

'Club Mystique.' Whispered the man. 'Nine o'clock.' He turned abruptly and walked off to the next ship across the large room.

Jared stormed off back towards the main entrance, his sausage fingers tapping erratically across his phone in his large hands. He exhaled heavily out of his quint nose and stopped suddenly spinning to look directly at James, his face stern and morose.

'Tonight, you may need to use your new toy.' He whispered seriously. His dark eyes boring into James's. He nodded then walked over to the large entrance as the crowds parted before his muscular build.

*

Jared and James arrived outside the heaving venue, it was only 20:30PM but already a long queue stood along the outside wall cordoned off by black rope and brass bollards fencing in the groups of skinny underdressed girls and swaying men who had visibly already had too many drinks. Jared strode for the door as the large bouncer flashed a gold toothed smile and nodded him and James inside. 'Evening Monsieur Araignée.'

'Privileges of the occupation.' Smiled Jared as they passed the fifty indignant people still waiting in the queue.

Purple, blue and pink neon lights strobed vibrantly over the hundreds of dancing heads as brilliant white fingers lanced and flashed blindingly across the room from the corners of the cosy small venue. Star shapes and text reading, "Welcome to Club Mystique" projected over the walls. The bass from the dance music hit James's chest and ears like a fist. Looking across to the small stage James could see two skinny white males stood behind the DJ set, bopping and twitching in time with the extremely loud music, a padded headphone earpiece held to one ear as the other hung free around their tiny necks. Above the packed dance floor, a narrow walkway ran the length of one of the walls, throngs of dancers adorned it like, their arms, hands and drinks hanging over like garlands along the metal railing.

Behind him the bar was four people thick, all leaning in against each other fighting for the stressed bar staff's attention. The few tables and chairs situated nearby were occupied with glassy eyed youths, rowdy stag and hen parties and local ravers downing shot after shot from their tables. Jared walked to the corner of the room nearest the narrow walkway and leant against the railing. His large, shaved and scar covered head scanning the building's occupants from left to right. *"Like the Terminator,"* though James to himself hiding a half smile.

'There!' snapped Jared as he touched his throat. 'Contact blue suit, four-man escort.' He bellowed over the thumping music and crowds cheers. James could hear Jared's voice clearly and undisturbed in his ear through the tiny earpiece he had been given before they entered the venue. As Jared spoke, he also saw a dozen people situated around the room dip their heads before nodding and touching their ears. All then looked over to the Chinese man who had just entered, blue suit, looked very expensive. Four large men surrounded him as they crossed the busy dance floor in unison.

'Is that Chen?' asked James.

Jared nodded silently, his eyes glaring as he watched the scene below them. Tapping his throat once more he called out 'Confirm coverage...' to which James again heard clearly in his earpiece.

Another crackle in his ear then James could hear, *"Confirmed, live feed in progress. We have eyes on."*

James watched as Chen and his entourage entered the door at the rear of the club. Moments later he saw the unmistakable She Hulk female forms of Rugen and Mino enter behind them. James looked beside him as Jared's knuckles whitened as he squeezed the railings. His teeth were bare and grinding.

"Move in." ordered an unknown voice through their earpieces.

'I want this area secured in two minutes, people. Keep the music playing.' Spat Jared tapping his throat. 'Weapons live, but I want all suspects detained and compliant if possible. Let's go.'

James watched as a dozen people around the room began ushering the members of the public towards the exits. The Orion operatives moved quickly, some had Dutch police badges, others just used brute force. One man pointed a gun at the two DJ's ordering them to keep the deafening music blaring. The club was emptying quickly as James and Jared walked towards the rear door where Chen, Rugen and Mino had just used. Jared and several others unholstered their firearms, raising them up aiming for the door as they approached. James pulled out his silenced Jericho 941 and followed them.

The door opened as a single Chinese man walked out with a cigarette in his mouth, lighting it as he looked up. The look on his face was of sheer confusion as the busy club that had been only minutes before, filled with hundreds of revellers. Was now an empty dance floor. It had been replaced with several figures walking towards him with weapons trained on him. The door shut behind him knocking him forward, his eyes opened wide as he reached for the pistol concealed within his jacket, his forehead exploded silently into thousands of specks of fleshy pulp. Red liquid sprayed the door frame turning different colours as the disco lighting reflected off of it as it dripped down the door and wall around him. The cigarette still stuck out of his frozen mouth, smoke plumed out of the hole above his nose, the face all but gone. The near headless figure slumped against the wall falling to the side as Jared moved in to open the door, it led into a long windowless corridor with several other doors leading off of it.

The pounding music and flashing lights were distracting, a barrage on the senses making James feel uneasy and disorientated. He lifted his gun and walked up behind Jared as the music suddenly and unexpectedly stopped. His ears still ringing from the exposure he turned around to look at the DJ booth atop the small stage. Chen's chauffeur and six others stood there, each holding a QBZ-191 assault rifle. Four more stood by the entrance and nearly a dozen had taken position along the narrow walkway above them.

James's heart stopped, his jaw quivered, and his hands shook violently. 'Jared!' he bellowed as the firing started. Muzzle flashes and shots erupted all around him as he ducked behind the nearest table. The metal body and top of the table pinged repeatedly as bullets ricochet off. Jared had launched into action whilst James had taken cover. He fired at the stage lighting rig above them taking out the nearest lights and the majority of the spotlights and strobes around them plunging the venue into darkness. His next shots were directed at the DJ booth causing the six men and the chauffeur to take cover as they returned fire over the top of the mixing decks. James felt a strong hand pulling on his shoulder, heaving him up to his feet as he was pulled towards the opened door besides the headless figure. Sporadic muzzle flashes lit the dark room revealing the true extent of the chaotic devastation that was unfolding. Bodies were being ripped apart by the dozens of QBZ-191's from the elevated walkway and although the Orion team had managed to take out several attackers, they were severely outnumbered and outgunned. James was thrown towards the door as he ran forward blindly. He stumbled on the dead Chinese man's body causing him to spin into the door frame jarring his left shoulder. Jared was again behind him half dragging him along the windowless corridor as he returned fire into the dark dance floor behind them.

'Move your blerrie backside kiddo!' roared Jared as they pushed through to a side door into a small office. The room had two desks back-to-back and ancient looking computers that had yellowed with age. Several filing cabinets ran along the wall below a small window. Sounds of firing ceased from the other end of the corridor and all went quiet. Jared winced as he held his thighs, his black t-shirt stained dark and wet across the back. 'Out of the window now!' he spat as he threw one of the ancient PC monitors from the desk beside them out through the small window sending glass shards everywhere. The sound of approaching footsteps rang out from the corridor behind them. James and Jared jumped down from the window into a narrow street filled with bins and recycling containers. The smell of stale beer and urine filled their lungs.

'Where's the rest of the team, Jared?' asked James. His face and eyes matching that of a rabbit in the headlights.

'Just keep moving.' He retorted, dragging him along. He pulled out his phone and hit a button pressing it to his blood splattered ear and cheek. 'Control! We were set up.'

"Where is Chen?" came the soft German voice of Number Two.

'He left with Rugen and Mino…' he winced again as he rolled his bloodied shoulder.

"Where are they now?" again came the soft German voice of Number Two. *"Do you have eyes on?"*

'Negative…' He paused as they reached a bustling street beside a canal filled with restaurants, their customers all sat beneath parasols dining and drinking in tranquillity. Unbeknownst to them that twenty people had just been butchered not thirty metres away. He looked up at a lamppost catching his breath, a small black orb was positioned beneath the light itself. 'The CCTV coverage, did they see Chen leaving?'

There was a pause, the silence seeming to take an age then, *"We are looking at it now."* Then another pause. *"Chen was seen getting into a black MPV with Rugen and Mino."*

'Any direction of travel?' spat Jared as he holstered his pistol and rubbed his shoulder.

"East" said the voice. *"Along Smaksteeg to Westerdokstraat."* There was some muffled speech in the background as if she were speaking to someone else and pressing the phone against their chest, then, *"We believe they are heading back towards-"*

'Westpoort!' snapped Jared as he punched the wall in frustration.

*

Jared pulled the steering wheel hard to the left sending the large INKAS Armoured Range Rover tail end out with a squeal as the 5.0 supercharged V8 engine launched them around the evening traffic along the A5. Unlike their last 4x4 that had suffered heavily during their mission detaining Chen's chauffeur, this time they had decided to use Orion's state of the art safety vehicle normally reserved for *Number One*'s personal travel. The luxurious vehicle was equipped with 360-perimeter protection up to CEN BR6 level of armour.

Jared looked sickly pale and had not stopped sweating since they'd left the club, but his determination and frustration was driving him on, he like many old soldiers had an amazing ability of harnessing anger as an energy. One that was far more powerful than excitement or adrenaline. James sat in the back with Maekin as another unknown male sat beside Jared up front. Maekin was loading a customised Heckler & Koch AG36 assault rifle single-shot 40 mm grenade launcher. He turned and nodded at James before returning to his rifle, checking the scope and lenses. The male in the front pulled out a huge AA-12 fully automatic shotgun affixing a specialised 20-round drum magazine filled with 12-gauge explosive shotgun shells.

Their large vehicle pulled up alongside the silent warehouse as the man up front jumped out running off towards the shadows of the corrugated metal wall. Jared drove a little further up the road as Maekin pulled himself out with a grunt giving James a little wink. James poked his head out of the rear passenger window. The night was calm and warm, James could hear the water hitting the harbour walls and faint 'ting-ting-ting' of the mast ropes from several small vessels moored along the harbour. Not a sound was coming from inside the warehouse but that was about to change.

Jared revved the powerful engine and drove it at the warehouse's futile security gate, the small security booth was vacant, and the gates flimsy red and white pole shattered as the Range Rover's reinforced bull bar tore through it as if it were made of balsa wood. He kept his foot down until they were beside a transit van some twenty metres from the entrance. They had made an effective roadblock should anyone try to leave. He turned and shouted back at James, 'Get your head down and shoot anything that comes at us.'

Seconds later James heard voices, lots of voices. Shouting and screaming in Chinese. A set of double doors burst open as dozens of Chinese men in suits ran out. Each carrying a QBZ-191 assault rifle.

James ducked as something erupted behind him, a cacophony of pops hurt his ears as the first wave of Chen's men were torn apart. James peaked out behind them to see the unknown man with the AA-12 smiling as he reloaded another drum. His previous 20 rounds were eaten up in under four seconds. The sound of tyres screeching from somewhere beside them made them all look over as two large MPVs sped towards them. The first vehicle stopped side on as six figures jumped out taking cover behind their vehicle, assault rifles resting along the long bonnet and top of the MPV as they opened fire at Jared and James. The second vehicle screeched a little further up, even closer to Jared and James' Range Rover. But then it erupted in a ball of flames as Maekin released the high explosive UGL grenade round as it utterly annihilated the front vehicle. The occupants didn't even have time to open the doors, let alone think about escaping. Maekin then released a heavy volley from his AG36 on the first vehicle before reloading the grenade launcher and releasing it towards the remaining MPV. There was no denying that this weapon was truly devastating and effective.

Jared and James climbed out and made their way to the double doors, Jared picked up one of the fallen QBZ-191 assault rifles and held it tight to his shoulder. He walked inside and released several blasts in two round bursts taking down more of Chen's men as he advanced.

James was flanked by Maekin and the unknown man as they too entered the warehouses' main structure. Inside was a vast complex of racking and aisles filled high with parts and crates. Along one side ran a series of small clinical cuboid offices and a metal stairwell that led up over the top of them off into the distance over the racking. James watched as Jared moved from one aisle to the next, his eyes scanning every inch of the area before he moved forward. Jared continued forward as one of

Chen's men dropped down from the racking above. He was holding what looked like a cleaver or watermelon knife, its 12-inch blade flickered as he pulled it up and back over his shoulder ready to strike into Jared's spine. James raised his Jericho and snapped off a round into the knifeman's shoulder making him drop the cleaver as Jared spun at the sound. Jared pulled out his own hunting knife and drove it hard into the man's neck just above his clavicle. He gave a nod to James and continued into the dark belly of the warehouse.

Several heads poked up from inside the cuboid offices as more of Chen's men released several shots smashing the office windows. The unknown man dropped to one knee and released the fury of the AA-12 as its explosive rounds shredded the offices plasterboard walls and remaining glass. The once white clinical stud walls now spattered red and black amid hundreds of bore holes.

Ahead of them a machine sprung into life as a huge industrial yellow forklift truck lifted its mighty forks to waist height and rolled towards them. It resembled a robotic yellow mammoth rampaging through the warehouse between the aisles. James and Jared both released several shots at the driver, but the machines thick safety glass just cobwebbed from the impacts. The driver sneered as he raced towards them. Maekin bellowed 'Down!' as he released another high explosive UGL grenade round as it pinged into the solid metal frontage of the giant forklift. The machine juddered backwards several feet as the forks splintered off to the sides at bizarre angles. The cab and occupant practically disintegrated as it blasted upwards, and the machine popped and banged violently as the several batteries inside exploded. The racking either side of the giant machine then groaned in protest as the blast impact twisted the frames as the stock flew from the shelves. The huge forklift then erupted into a final catastrophic blast as the six large gas canisters at the rear, and pistons within exploded. The thirty-foot-high racking began to fall like ribbed dominos in noisy cascades away from the shattering thundering blast as the impact from one caused the next to buckle and also fall. The lights then flickered and went out as the bulb housings above the explosion fizzed and sparked menacingly. The warehouse now fell into complete darkness lit only by the flames of the burning carcass of the gnarled giant forklift.

Jared, James and the unknown man turned to look at Maekin with a concerned look as the racking finally stopped falling around them.

'What?' replied Maekin as he reloaded his rifle with a sniff.

The four of them continued through the now ruined warehouse until they arrived at the rear of the structure. The next section of the humongous building was similar to an airport hangar and unlike the previous section this had been cleared of racking and now housed hundreds of stacked crates all standing in the centre under several rows of strip lighting. These evidently being fed from a separate generator as they illuminated the arranged crates in beams of orange. Some of the crates were open and James saw the contents from their vantage point by the large doorway. Each crate contained dozens of small packages filled with white powder. Some had dark powder and some crates contained larger bags of green plant leaves. Several smaller crates contained assault rifles and ammunition boxes.

On the opposite end of the hangar building stood thirty men and two women. All taking cover behind the wall of crates and some more racking that flanked the rear walls. All of them had their weapons pointed at Jared and James.

'It's over Chen!' called Jared from the darkness. His eyes counted the opposition that were thankfully illuminated, but he knew they were outnumbered.

A series of rounds replied to him as they all took cover in the doorway. Jared looked to Maekin and the other man as they nodded. 'James keep your head down, leave this to us.'

They poked around the edges of the large doorway unleashing everything they had at Chen and his men across the towering void of crates. James held his palms against his ears at the deafening sound as he knelt behind the door frame. Each shot echoed resoundingly throughout the warehouse and hangar area.

Silence fell as both sides waited for something to happen, James stood up making his way to Jared's shoulder as he chanced a glimpse through the nearby window that looked out to the exterior of the warehouse. The silence was broken with the distinct sound of a large roller door being opened somewhere in the warehouse as it echoed through the expanse.

'They're making a run for it!' spat James as he pointed outside at Chen and Mino running through the now open hanger door.

He watched in horror as they managed to get several paces before they became illuminated by a giant spotlight from above. The warehouse was now filled with the deafening engines of the sleek Boeing AH-64 Apache as it roared intimidatingly above them. The airborne tank lowered to hover just above them. It greeted them with its menacing ensemble of overwhelming destructive firepower that had been assorted onto this flying death machine. This bird was not to be underestimated and Chen knew it. He stopped and raised his hands; his normally slick hair now being thrown about by the turbulent wind from the large propellor above. Mino screamed up in defiance at the helicopter as she pulled out a pistol from the

small of her back and began firing at the armoured fuselage as the two occupants of the AH-64 returned the courtesy. Mino was shredded by a sudden burst of 50. Calibre tracer fire rounds that thumped their way effortlessly through her torso pock marking the concrete floor around her as if she wasn't even there. What was left of her mutilated body fell heavily to the ground as dark red pooled all around her ravaged remains.

Chen ducked and held his head as the helicopter turned a few degrees to stare at him, he dropped to his knees and held his hands and arms even higher. Rugen walked out from the dark hangar and threw her pistol to the ground. She knelt beside Mino's corpse and began sobbing loudly, her back arching and shoulders dropping with each retching cry. Chen's dozen remaining men all filed out into the blinding spotlight of the Apache helicopter, their arms held high and heads down submissively. Behind them were their escorts. Jared, James, Maekin and the unknown man.

Jared waved at the pilot and held his throat as he spoke. 'Glad you could make it.' He smiled weakly. 'Site is secure.' Called Jared as he limped back inside to sit on one of the drugs filled boxes. His face was even paler than before, his top sodden with sweat and blood. He put down his weapon and held the rear of his neck wincing.

He looked up as Number Two walked over to him from beneath the helicopter as dozens of armed people encircled Chen and his men. 'Well done Monsieur Araignée.' She smiled defiantly as her team rounded up Chen and his men transferring them into waiting vehicles. 'And well done to you Mr Bond.' she remarked at the sweating teenager.

'Jared… get yourself seen to. I don't want to lose my best man.' She smiled as she walked into the warehouse followed by more of Orion's people. 'Secure the drugs, lock this place down.' She beamed as she shouted at her people as they scurried around her securing the site.

*

That evening James helped Jared into the apartment, he hadn't realised just how heavy Jared was until he had to physically drag him up the last few steps. James had found the number for Jared's emergency medic in the small black book beside the telephone and having explained what had happened a young doctor arrived thirty minutes after. She was beautiful, short, petite, dark skinned with large bright eyes and a smile that made you feel better just by seeing it. James left her to it as he fell into his bed, he heard Jared moaning a few times but thought it best not to get in the way. The next morning Jared was sitting at his dining table as the stunning female doctor stood behind him changing the dressings she had applied the evening before on his many wounds. The neck injury was healing, she had said. But his back and shoulder looked awful. The gauze was sodden and thick with fresh blood and Jared looked awful. Physically he looked terrible, his face was at least three shades paler than usual, and he hadn't stopped sweating since the previous evening.

'There is something in the wound and it will become contaminated and infected if not dealt with immediately.' Started the doctor as she peeled off another gauze strip, 'I will need to take it out so the blood can coagulate and we can stabilise the soft tissue, but he has already lost too much blood.'

Jared sat up straight and looked her in the eye, 'No hospital.' James could see his hands shaking and his lips had gone an off purple-blue colour.

'What do you need from the hospital?' asked James. 'I can bring what you need here.' He said with a smile.

'He needs a blood transfusion, saline, morphine… I need everything… Cannula's and a surgical stapler.' She shook her head indignantly as she checked Jared's shredded back.

'Just make me a list and I will get everything.' Reassured James with a broad smile.

'And just how, young man do you expect to get all of this equipment?' she raised an eyebrow.

*

James walked through the storeroom of The University of Amsterdam's AMC Faculty of Medicine. He knew what most of the items on the doctors list were but some he had never heard of. He had filled his large kit bag with everything on there but now all he needed was blood for Jared's transfusion. He made his way through the corridors of the building until he found what he was looking for. An active lab with samples and more importantly, blood. He waited for the young man in the white lab coat to turn back to a large white machine that looked like it belonged in Star Trek before he walked in. Making his way to the store at the far end he pushed his way through into the clinical room, and it was cold, freezing actually, purposefully so as to preserve the samples and contents of the experiments. He opened a fridge, 'Nope…' he said to no one as he tried a few more. Then finally he had found it. *"Type B - RhD positive"* he grabbed four bags, some tubing and specialist IV cannulas into his kit bag.

'Hey, what are you doing in there?' shouted a voice from behind him.

James spun to find the young man in the white lab coat standing behind him. And he didn't look very happy to see him.

James cleared his throat and stepped forward. 'Dr *Eijkman* sent me up to collect some samples…' replied James calmly as he forced a smile. The young man glared at him for a minute then nodded. He turned and walked out of the chilled storeroom before pushing the door closed and locking it from outside. Trapping James inside.

The young man ran to the nearest telephone and dialled a number, 'Security to Lab 3… We have an intruder.'

James looked around and swore loudly. 'Now what do I do?' he whispered to himself. He tried the door, but it wouldn't move. It was designed for one purpose, and it did this purpose very well. He turned and looked around the room. No other doors, one window but it was locked tight, barred and he was pretty sure he was on the second floor. He looked around him to see what else was in the room. James smiled as he picked up a small beaker and ran to one of the Cryo Storage units opening the lid. He pulled on some of the heavy-duty gloves and grabbed the long tongs and lowered the beaker inside. He pulled up the beaker to find it was frozen solid as it shattered under the pressure of the tongs. He swore again then decided to spare the delicacies as he lifted the entire 10 litre Cryostorage unit barrel and carried it awkwardly towards the security door. He poured the contents onto the doors lock and middle panel as the glass crunched and the thin metal beading groaned. He carried on pouring out the liquid solution as it emitted the familiar dragon's breath cloud of white smoke as the liquid nitrogen boiled into nitrogen vapour at room temperature. He threw the now empty barrel across the room and readied himself. With a swift front kick the security doors lock buckled as the heavy door swung open. He stepped out as the young man in the lab coat backed off with arms raised in submission.

'That wasn't very nice now, was it?' asked James as he re-shouldered the kit bag and made his way past the cowering technician and out of the lab. As he reached the bottom of the stairs two burly and (judging by their excessive panting) very unfit security guards ran towards him. James smiled and pointed up the stairs.

'Thank you for coming so quickly, the intruder you are after is wearing a white lab coat… Up there.' He smiled as they nodded thankfully and ran up past him. James walked out of the campus smiling, he truly felt alive. A world away from the troubled and challenging days of Fettes. He suddenly realised that since the previous night he hadn't felt nervous or apprehensive. He looked down to his hands marvelling at how steady they were. He began to exude and feel a confidence that he had lost when his parents had died. He looked up at the beautiful sky and inhaled deeply before sprinting back towards Jared's apartment.

The procedure went very well, and the doctor advised that after lots of rest Jared should make a full recovery. It transpired that he had two rounds of the QBZ-191 in his shoulder, one was complete and the other had fragmented but she was certain she had removed all of the shrapnel pieces. She jokingly asked if James would be able to visit the radiography suite to acquire an x-ray generator and detector to bring back to Jared's apartment.

After breakfast Jared handed her a thick pile of Euro notes, kissed her and thanked her again before she left them alone. James continued to watch over Jared for the next two days after they had both been given leave. James enjoyed this special time he spent with Jared. It reminded him of past holidays he'd taken with his uncle Max and aunt Charmian. Although Jared refused to be a burden and protested to be waited on, he did appreciate the young man's help with cooking the meals and reporting back to Orion Control when they called. Business was going well, and James finally felt as though he knew his place.

*

Chapter 9

The Fall

Orion Command Room, Amsterdam.

'Orion's Amsterdam office has made over €400 million profit this year. And we just seized approximately €20 - €30 million of Chen's merchandise... That is the current street value.' Said a severe looking man with a slim bird-like face and deep dark eyes from the centre of the long conference table to the congregation around him.

Number One clicked his control panel as a series of charts similar to stock tables and the FTSI were displayed over all the surrounding screens of the Command Room. It showed the fluctuating prices of the drug market and the current street value.

DRUG	AVERAGE (CURRENT) PRICE
Amphetamine per gram	€5 upwards
Cocaine per gram	€45-70
CRACK (per rock)	€15-25
Diazepam per pill	€0.75c - €1
Ecstasy per pill	€10-20
Herbal cannabis (standard) per qtr oz	€40

Herbal cannabis (high strength) per qtr oz	€60
Ketamine per gram	€200 +
Heroin per bag – average bag weight 0.1g	€15
MDMA powder/crystal per gram	€50
Methamphetamine per gram	€200 +
Spice	€45-70 (LONDON) / €30 FOR 3.5g

'Chen was looking to push through the city and flood the market with cheaper lower grade drugs.' Continued the slim man to *Number One*. 'Mino and Rugen were prepared to distribute his filth via our coffee shops, vendors and agents.' The thin man stopped as the door opened causing all the assembled men to look over. Number Two walked in, her face visibly indignant and agitated. She scowled around the room before approaching *Number One* with a small head bow.

'Forgive the interruption, but we need to talk...' She looked up at the monitors then back to *Number One* with a frown. 'Still preparing for Operation Botox I see. Very good.'

'What is it you need Number Two?' asked her superior, his eyes not meeting hers.

'Rugen has started talking...' the old German pursed her lips together as she paused. 'We administered the Sodium Pentothal and she is now opening up.' A man sat at the table coughed as he removed his Fedora hat and loosened his shirt collar as he looked towards *Number Two*.

'What has she said?' asked the Fedora man. 'Have we learnt anything yet?'

Number Two eyed the man a little taken aback. The audacity of his tone made her uncomfortable. 'Number Five…' she said with a nod. 'Just nonsensical words at this time. The solution will take a little more time.' replied Number Two turning back to Number One.

'Yes, that is brilliant news. Let me know the moment she gives up a name.' smiled *Number One*. He remained silent almost too long. Tension and unease filled the large room until Number Two got the message and left the room shaking her head indignantly.

'She is tenaciously devoted to the cause…' snapped Fedora man.

Number One sneered, as the security door slammed behind her. 'It is a shame really.' He stood and walked around the room as the assorted gentlemen followed him with their eyes.

'We will begin phase three sooner than anticipated. Any questions?' His eyes scanned the room as all present remained silent. 'Excellent. Now we need to eliminate any loose ends.' He said nonchalantly as he pulled out his revolver, shooting two of the men seated beside him in quick succession.

'Congratulations on your promotion from Number Five to Number Three.' sneered Number One as the man put his Fedora back on his head with a beaming grin.

'Release the order on Number Two and bring me Monsieur Araignée and his little protégée James Bond.'

*

'At last!' exclaimed Jared as he pulled himself up gingerly out of the chair. He pocketed his mobile phone and smiled. 'We're back in action kiddo.'

James watched his friend standing then shook his head, 'You sure you're ready?' he laughed playfully. 'It has only been two days.'

'Dumbkopf! I was born ready.' Jeered Jared as he flexed his large arm muscles. James narrowed his eyes, throwing the television remote at Jared who twisted to catch it. 'Argh!!' he whimpered as he tried to stand back upright. His back and shoulder throbbing once more as he sucked his teeth in frustration.

'You are nowhere near ready,' James stood to help his friend. 'If they want you back you need to be able to protect yourself.' Taking his proffered arm, he aided him over to the kitchen area. 'I think you should give it another few days, just to be sure.'

Jared took more of the painkillers left behind by his personal medic and swallowed them down with a mouthful of water. His phone rang in his pocket as he nodded to James, 'Maybe you're right kiddo.'

He answered the phone as his smile fell. 'Number Two?' he frowned, 'Is that you?'

*

James opened the apartment door to find a dishevelled Number Two leaning against the wall. Her immaculate hair was tousled and straggled as if she had been dragged through some bushes. The makeup on her usually flawless face had been smudged around her bloodshot eyes, her lips thin and stressed. Her clothes were scuffed at the knees and the shirt blouse torn at the collar and appeared scorched in places. She gripped her handbag over her shoulder, her other hand gripped a small pistol.

'Ma'am?' asked James as he moved aside for her to enter. She pushed past him making a beeline across the apartment to Jared.

Jared stood tall and focused behind the breakfast bar with his strong arms propped up before him holding him up, his previous signs of weakness and injury all but gone. He looked her up and down and narrowed his dark eyes. He was about to speak before she cut him off with a raised hand.

'We don't have time…' she spat. '*Number One* has played us all. We are all of us in grave danger.' She winced as she pulled out a small tablet from her handbag. The screen showed pictures of a dozen faces in both colour and black and white. James could clearly see that he and Jared were two of faces amongst the dozens. 'We need to lay low, and we need all the help we can get.'

James ran to his room, gathered up his belongings and holstered his pistol. He took out his mobile phone and shut the bedroom door. *"We need all the help we can get."* He said to himself as he recalled Number Two's words clearly. He tapped several keys and held the phone to his ear as it began to ring.

Outside the apartment Jared was loading his bag into the boot of the INKAS Armoured Range Rover as Number Two sat behind the wheel with the engine running. James walked over and threw his kit bags inside and clambered in the rear passenger seat.

They made their way to the outskirts of town as the city continued on outside oblivious to the trauma that was about to befall it.

Number Two brushed the loose hair behind her ear as she drove them far from the centre of town. James didn't recognise the area at all, but he thought it best not to ask trivial questions considering that they had just had to leave Jared's safe house as they continued their escape and evasion.

'It transpires that *Number One* has been playing everyone along, with an ulterior motive being undertaken that none of us were aware of. His original plan has worked perfectly, thus far... But I intend to compromise him.' She drove into a small car park and turned off the headlights. She turned in her seat to face Jared and James before she continued. 'Phase one was to remove the burden of the criminal justice offspring within London, a trial to see the potency and effectiveness to then be carried out around all major European cities, but we had all been distracted with the task of identifying and locating Chen. Number One then created the illusion of a mole within our organisation, and with your arrival this was easily believed.' she said to James. 'In the process Number One has also managed to instigate Mino and Rugen who had actually been sent undercover on the assumption that they were going to find said mole. Phase two was to take down Chen, confiscate and destroy his drugs, which you two performed perfectly by the way. He then took out Mino and Rugen labelling them as the moles.' She stopped talking as a car drove past them. She pulled out her pistol and watched as the old man inside continued further into the car park, not even acknowledging they were there.

'Phase three is where things become problematic for all of us. *Number One* had no intention of destroying Chen's drug supply or of tainting Orion's own supply to eradicate the predicament of uncontrollable drug supply, use and addiction pandemic that is poisoning our world. The sole purpose of Project Tabula Rasa.' She looked physically hurt by this, James could see the disappointment and sadness in her eyes.

'Let me guess…' started James. 'He intends to become the 'Il Capo dei Capi', the top dog of narcotics and organised crime in Europe.'

Number Two looked at the teenager sheepishly. 'Exactly.' she replied, chagrined and crestfallen. 'There are orders out to exterminate us all and shift the entire Orion project into the one thing we have been trying to stop and fight for years.'

'And what do you intend to do?' asked Jared calmly. 'Or should I say what do you need us to do?'

James sat in silence as Number Two and Jared discussed their intended plan in so much detail it began to make James' head hurt.

Jared and James walked into the terraced row of buildings opposite the Hortus Botanicus Amsterdam as they made sure they looked up at as many of the CCTV cameras as possible without making it too obvious that they wanted to be seen by Orion. Like the first time James visited the main head office for Orion the large door opened as they approached.

Again, the dozens of CCTV cameras watched their every move. James and Jared were escorted into the shiny steel elevator by two large men, James noticed that this time they were visibly armed. Jared pushed the button and the door slid silently closed. Their escorts didn't say a word making their descent more imposing. Jared dropped to his right knee as he fiddled with the lace of his left boot discreetly placing a small disc against the magnetic side of the elevator cabin. Approximately 20 seconds later the door slid open revealing the huge brightly lit underground chamber dotted with the dozens of small international offices that ran each side of the vast room. Each office now sat empty, the flat screen monitors dormant and dark.

The far wall housed the large security door leading to the main control room where they were to meet *Number One*. The way was again guarded by the two bald-headed men who moved forward to frisk them before they were allowed entry, removing their phones and firearms.

They entered the cavernous room to see *Number One* standing behind the long conference table flanked by half a dozen suited brutes perched in the matching Fritz Hansen egg chairs in black leather and chrome bases. The old man was silent as he stood watching the large monitors spanning the one-hundred-foot square walls. It was not until Jared coughed that he half turned, eyeing them up and down before returning his gaze at the monitors.

'I have been waiting for you two…' he spoke softly, still not diverting his gaze from the large monitor. He stalked back to the tactical Alpha Command Chair as he tapped one of the slim monitor control panels on the chair arm. 'One seldom expects to wait, especially for the likes of you two.' He glared at them as he inhaled heavily like an indignant bull before returning his eyes up to the monitors.

'Number Two has gone rogue; I fear she was the one behind Rugen and Mino's treachery.' He continued. His words were gentle and delicate as if he was talking about something trivial like a comment on the weather. 'I want you to help me track her down and terminate her.' His cold eyes now staring directly at them.

'What happened to the plan?' asked Jared diplomatically, raising his eyebrow. 'I thought we always stuck to the plan?'

'Plans change... People change. One must always be ready and flexible to instil a contingency. They say, *"To err is human"* Monsieur Araignée,' sneered *Number One* maliciously. 'But *we* do not allow errors in Orion.' He stood away from his chair and walked closer to them, running his fingers idly along the smooth cold surface of the conference table. 'New plan, kill Number Two and aid us with the next phase of Orion's future.'

'And what is the future of Orion?' asked James seriously. Jared held up a hand to stop him speaking but he pushed forward. 'What have you lined up for this next phase?'

Number One laughed heartily as he turned to the others sitting at the table, 'Why it is simply World manipulation through the vices of the weak.'

'And the promise of putting a stop to organised crime, drug dealing, human trafficking?' huffed James. The old man just stood there staring at him smiling, his dead eyes revealing their true psychopathic intentions.

'My child... Why would we want to stop what we already control?' he laughed maniacally as the others around the table joined in.

'This was not the ethos of Orion.' Sighed Jared, shaking his head morosely. 'The objective was to destroy the sordid criminal world from within. What changed?'

'This is the future gentlemen...' started *Number One*. 'Join us as we ascend to a pious level, where Orion will rule over these mere mortal men.' He said pointing up at the monitors showing news broadcasts of politicians and police forces from around the globe.

'And if we refuse to cooperate with this madness?' asked James bluntly. 'What then?'

'I would have thought that obvious Mr Bond… Monsieur Araignée must have made our strict processes quite evident to you?' his eyes slitted between the two of them before his thin lips curled into a sinister grin, 'I expect you to die Mr Bond.'

'I'd rather live today, and die tomorrow if it's all the same to you.' retorted James, making Jared half-smile.

'And this has come from the top?' questioned Jared interrupting him. 'Have the other world offices of Orion authorised this action? Or is this some kind of internal coup d'état?'

The old man gnarled his top lip as he shouted, 'You will answer to MY authority!' he spat aggressively slamming his hand down on the table. 'I am Orion!' he bellowed. 'I am the only authority!'

'Authority is there to be questioned.' Retorted James bitterly.

Jared pushed him back as his large dark eyes narrowed to an almost closed squint.

'And I thought you were a smart man… Goodbye Mr Bruce… Goodbye Mr Bond. Kill them both.' Waved *Number One* nonchalantly as one of the men stood behind them raised his pistol; it was Maekin.

*

'SIR!' shouted a voice from the meeting room doorway making them all turn with a start, 'Sir we have contact outside the facility. Our perimeter has been breached.' Shouted the alarmed voice.

Number One ran to his control panel command chair hitting several buttons as the largest monitor affixed to the wall flicked to the CCTV view of the street. The image shone downwards to reveal a rotund figure dressed all in black tactical clothing standing on the street firing up at the top of the building. *Number One* looked at another screen then back up to the figure as it turned to point their gun up at the camera watching him before the screen turned to static.

'Sir he appears to be disabling the security cameras.' Came the alarmed voice.

Number One rolled his eyes angrily, 'I am aware of that you imbécile.' He held down a button as the tannoy clicked into life above them. The entire complex rang out with his domineering voice, 'All unit's code blue. Eliminate the hostile with all immediacy.' As he said this a loud claxon rang out throughout the compound.

The monitor flicked to another angle as the large intruder made his way into the building proper. The corridor was filled with Orion agents, but they all lay face down or prostrate as the intruder made his way through the building complex. 'What is happening?' spat *Number One* as the meeting room door rushed open once more.

Three men entered wearing full tactical gear, matt black Ops-Core Future Assault Shell Technology (FAST) Helmet with full face armoured riot visors all carrying Heckler & Koch HK416. One man held a full-length armoured riot ballistic shield. They stormed through the room surrounding *Number One* in a triangle formation as they strapped a bullet proof vest to him and started moving him away towards the rear of the room beside the large fireplace and antique writing desk.

'What about these two?' spat Maekin looking back at James and Jared, his pistol still raised.

'Shoot them both in the head and take care of that intruder.' He barked looking up as another CCTV camera lost its feed. *Number One* was ushered out of the room and into a long sloping dog legged corridor that led down to an underground car park where four more tactical geared male and female soldiers stood either side of one of the INKAS Range Rovers. He climbed in with them and opened the super thin laptop as two dozen images from all around the complex filled the high-definition screen. Half had now been turned to static as he looked to see what was transpiring above him. He grinned to himself as he saw four more heavily armoured and seriously armed soldiers enter the elevator as the door closed behind them. It began to climb up to ground level where the unsuspecting intruder was still causing absolute havok, but then the screen flashed brightly grabbing *Number One*'s undivided attention. He watched the scene play out in silence as it displayed the CCTV image as it unfolded in real time. The four men were thrown violently against the walls of the elevator as smoke filled the small metallic cabin. 'What!' he spat. 'What was that?' he cried in horror as the four soldiers sat around him looked at each other in silence.

*

Back inside the main control room Maekin cocked his pistol as *Number One* was ushered away out of the room. He waited for the door to close then sniffed, 'Now?' he asked unsurely over the deafening claxon.

Jared turned and nodded, 'Now!' he smiled, grabbing James and pulling him to the ground as Maekin shot the six well-dressed goons in suits still sitting around the conference table in quick succession. He handed Jared a small remote detonator before he spun on his heels and turned to the main door as the two bald headed men came crashing through as both their heads exploded. Maekin lowered his pistol and scanned the room. 'Clear!' he shouted to Jared and James who stood up to see the carnage.

Jared held up the remote detonator and smiled, 'Fire in the blerrie hole.' He pressed the button as a thunderous tinny sound filled the chamber causing the building to shake and the irritating claxon to suddenly stop. His eyes fixed to one of the monitors that showed the inside of the elevator they had just descended in. The four armoured men were thrown violently against the walls as smoke filled the elevator.

Jared ran to the nearest suited man and ripped open his jacket to retrieve the man's holstered pistol as James ran to take his Jericho and Jared's Beretta from the dead bald-headed guard who had frisked them. 'What are we going to do about *Number One*?' asked James cautiously.

*

Number One threw the ultra-thin laptop into the footwell and swore loudly as his vehicle raced out of the complex. Another vehicle was waiting for them at a set of thick rolling blast doors that led out onto the busy streets. They followed the other vehicle as they cascaded and drove around the civilian vehicles towards the airport.

'Where is my air support?' spat Number One looking up out of the nearest window trying to spot the Apache helicopter.

'One minute out Sir.' Replied one of the armoured soldiers just as their visor exploded in red juice and small lumps of fleshy pulp. The next two soldiers met the same fate as their heads instantly concaved inwards as a shower of dripping blood trickled down from their visors. *Number One's* eyes went wide with shock as he looked up to see the fourth soldier holding a small hand cannon, it was a modified Desert Eagle .50 calibre. The soldier took off her helmet to reveal the bruised face of Rugen smiling back at him.

*

Silvery wisps of smoke emitted from the gaps in the shiny modern elevator door as Jared opened the neighbouring original antique elevator door as James and Maekin climbed into the brass and wooden ribbed cage of the two-hundred-year-old cabins mechanism. He pulled the lever and selected the top floor as they started to climb. James was surprised at how fast the old elevator moved as they ascended.

The door opened to a scene of chaos, lights strobed and sparked, and the once smooth walls and architrave were littered and riddled with hundreds of bullet holes. Dozens of bodies lay all over the place, twisted and mangled in bizarre contortions. Some missing limbs and some missing heads or face's. Jared walked into the war zone as he shouted out, 'Max?'

A large figure walked out from behind one of the devastated walls, the large rotund chest made even bigger by a thick NIK Level IV bullet proof vest. The figure removed his balaclava to reveal James' uncle Max. His face glistening with sweat and chubby cheeks flushed a rosy red from the ordeal. 'It's best your Aunt Charmian never hears of this young James.' He said solemnly as he shouldered his assault rifle embracing his nephew tightly within his large free arm. 'I've missed you my boy.' He kissed the top of James's head and gave him a hard yet affectionate squeeze.

'We need to keep moving.' Called Jared as they walked through the ruined building back towards civilization. Peering out of the door Jared looked up and down the road, no one was in sight. Not surprisingly after what sounded like World War Three had just begun from within the ravaged carcass of the building complex. 'Police will be here in a matter of minutes.'

As he squinted up the road, he could hear the distinct wailing "wee-woar" characteristic of the Dutch Police approaching in the distance. They ran out across the road in a single column taking cover behind the trees for shelter when all of a sudden, a deafening thunder pounded them from above, buffeting their ears. Looking up they could see the Boeing AH-64 Apache roaring across the sky from behind one of the neighbouring buildings.

It had spotted them and to make things worse the Apache had four Hellfire missiles attached to the side of the underwing racking. At over $150,000 each The Hellfire is a devastating precision missile used to strike ground and maritime targets. At just over five feet long and seven inches wide each of them weighs approximately 100 pounds and could practically kill a heavily armoured tank at ranges of up to five miles. They were only thirty metres away and the Apache lowered its gunner's senor turret bobbled nose as the pilot took his aim with his 30mm chain gun.

'RUN!!' shouted Jared and Max as they sprinted through the world's oldest botanical gardens, the Hortus Botanicus Amsterdam. Jared knew this was not the best place to head due to the building being a ginormous green house with thousands of large glass panels across all the ceiling and walls, but it was better than no cover at all. The Apache released burst after burst of tracer fire as explosions of shattered pieces of glass rained down from overhead. The sound alone was terrifying as hundreds of panes of glass began popping and pinging as they clattered down on them whilst they ran through the exotic foliage and trees. Then everything went silent as they were all knocked sideways off their feet into the long grasses and large ferns. Ringing plagued their throbbing ears and smoke filled the normally moist green tranquil space. The Apache had released one of its Hellfire missiles hitting the top of the thin metal latticed structure of the Hortus Botanicus causing most of the flimsy meshed metal to collapse and fragment into a ball of flame before a wall of fragmented glass was shot out from the after explosion in a 360-degree shockwave.

*

'What are you going to do, Rugen?' asked *Number One* gingerly as he looked at the driver in the rear-view mirror. It was only then that he glimpsed the ponytail hidden under the hat. This was when he realised that the driver was none other than Number Two. They overtook the lead escort vehicle on the main road. The four soldiers inside were no doubt unaware of his predicament and with no way of signalling them they would not come to his aid as they accelerated past.

He smiled awkwardly as Rugen glared at him, her pistol perfectly still, her professional hands calm and fixed as the barrel trained on his heart. 'What do you want?' he pleaded, 'I can give you anything you want…' It was hopeless and he knew it. His cold eyes flitted from the barrel to her fixated eyes.

Rugen swallowed hard then leant forward as she whispered, 'I want Mino you piece of-'

BANG!

The INKAS Range Rover spun out as a huge explosion erupted behind them causing all three of them to lurch violently in their seats. The escort vehicle just behind them was no more than a flaming ball of metal. Rugen looked up to see the Apache tailing them as they continued along the main road. The airships chain gun ripped noisily as it released hundreds of rounds at the body of the armoured car, each round pinged and banged violently but none made it through the tough exterior of the INKAS.

Number One looked up concerned as to why his own helicopter had started firing on him only to see the entire cockpit canopy had been removed. Where the Gunner and Pilot would normally be situated instead was a large sweaty man dressed in black and Jared sat behind him in the higher pilot seat.

'What the f-'

*

James pushed himself up to his feet shaking his head as his ears continued to ring stridently. Looking above them, he could see the Apache circling around to see where they had gone, the dense smoke making it hard for them to be seen. The aircrafts night vision was useless in the middle of the day, and it wasn't as if the pilot could look down.

James sprinted to a nearby metal spiral staircase that led up to a thin glass bottomed walkway that ran the length of the botanical garden. Most of this glass pathway had now been shattered but that wasn't what he had in mind. Keeping himself behind the helicopter he moved up until he could reach and climb up onto one of the steel girders that webbed up and ribbed around the complex keeping what was left of the roof up. He waited for the helicopter to pass once more as he saw the Gunner's side window hinge open at the top at a 90-degree angle like a DeLorean. The helmeted figure poked his head out as the pilot behind him kept the helicopter steady just feet above the devastated glass ceiling. Looking down he could finally make out the shapes of Jared, Max and Maekin but what happened next nobody could have guessed.

The Gunner leant out as he started shouting into his mouthpiece at the pilot behind him when all of sudden a teenage boy jumped from the top of the glass structure and onto the side of the Apache that was hovering mere feet above it. The Gunner let out a scream at the unexpected sight making the pilot double take as he saw the young man's face come into the Gunner's open window before the young boy punched the Gunner violently in the throat making him gag into the mouthpiece before his head lulled forward now unconscious. James pulled out his pistol and pointed it at the rear pilot's face.

'LAND!' He bellowed over the din of the thundering rotors. He dipped his pistol to gesticulate the helicopter landing as the Pilot only looked on in horror.

James was acting on the spot, the adrenaline pulsing around his body was making his chest ache as his heart pounded so violently that he felt like he was about to vomit, but even more bizarrely was the fact that he relished it. The Pilot looked down at the glass ceiling then off to the grassed gardens below as he nodded in defeated acceptance.

As the aircraft began to lift the Pilot made a rapid, unexpected evasive manoeuvre by tipping the helicopter down nose first so quickly that James lost his hold with his one free hand, and he fell out of the Gunner's window. He managed to take hold of the raised night vision sensor on the tip of the aircraft's nose as he looked down at the forty foot drop below through broken glass and distorted mangled steel.

'James!' shouted a voice from below as he looked down to see Jared, Max and Maekin had followed suit and climbed up onto the precarious glass roof. James pulled himself up as the helicopter attempted to lift off and away from the ruined ceiling, but James' comrades had already made it close enough that Jared leapt forward through the open window looping his arm through the seatbelt harness of the unconscious Gunner. He pulled the hammer back on his pistol and pointed it at the Pilot.

'Two choices Draadtrekker… One, you land this bird right now. Or two… I kill you and your Hol naier friend right now!'

*

Chapter 10

The Fold

A9 Lijnden, Amsterdam.

Number Two slammed on the brakes as the Range Rover skidded to a halt. She opened the door and pulled off her hat letting her tangled hair fall free around her face. She held both hands out before stepping out of the driver's seat looking up at the hovering helicopter.

James and Maekin rolled up in a stolen panel van as Jared landed the helicopter in the middle of the main road. Jared and Max pulled *Number One* out of the Range Rover and threw him against the van before securing him with thick yellow cable tie restraints.

The old man turned and grinned as he looked Jared up and down, he began to laugh maniacally nodding his head. 'Well done…' he started lifting his bound hands up in front of him. He slipped a knife from within his jacket instantly releasing his hands from the plastic restraints before slashing Jared hard across the chest sending him recoiling backwards as Max stepped forward to tackle the knife from his grip. Max punched the old man hard in the mouth sending his head rebounding off the side of the panel van as he hollered in agony.

'You!!' spat *Number One* through bloodied teeth. 'I know your face,' he paused for a second before lunging forward attempting a slash to Max's chest, then stuck the knife in hard to Max's shoulder with a sinister smile. Max looked up and head butted the old man back into the van. His thick body armour had taken the brunt of the blade allowing only a millimetre of metal to penetrate. Max retorted with a series of shattering blows to the face that shook the old man who fell to his knees.

'I thought I'd taken care of you and your brother all those years ago.' Sneered Number One, touching his bloodied nose gingerly. 'He left his mark,' tapping the indentation on his left temple, 'Now I shall leave my own on you.' He spat blood into Max's eyes making him recoil backwards. The two men engaged gripping one another's lapels like grappling Greek wrestlers, each trying to topple the other and claim the victory. Spilling down to the floor Max put the older man into a guillotine head lock and applied pressure, another few seconds and the old man would pass out as the blood flow ceased to his head. But he wasn't going to let that happen. The old man pulled out a short triangular blade from his belt and plunged it into Max's thigh before twisting the blade 90 degrees. Max roared as he released the head lock and placed both hands either side of the protruding knife as the old man clambered to his feet coughing and retching for breath. Drop kicking Max in the chest dropping him to his side in a foetal position.

Number One stepped forward, placing his legs either side of Max as a small fist came flying in from his left, dropping him hard to the ground. He looked up in a daze to see James standing there shaking his aching fist. James helped Max stand offering a shoulder under his uncles' arm. Max hobbled over the fallen old man and whispered, 'Now it's my turn.' Max clobbered the old man hard in the side of the face with his large fist as Number One's eyes glazed over. Max shuffled on his feet and held his injured leg as he winced. 'Stand back boy and look away.' He said firmly as he pulled the pistol out of James' belt and pushed him away. 'You don't want to see this part.'

Max dropped a knee on his good leg, keeping the injured leg straight as he slid the pistol's barrel under the old man's chin. 'Unlike my brother, *I* will not fail!' Shouted Max raising his pistol up to the old man's left temple. His barrel pushed into the deep scarred indentation as he pulled back the hammer with his large thumb.

'Stop!' called James from behind them. 'Not like this Max...' James placed a hand on his uncle's shoulder giving it a squeeze through the body armour. 'We need to let the authorities-'

'No James.' Said Max, cutting him off. 'If you only knew what this man has done.' He again pushed the barrel hard into the hollow of the old man's temple.

'Be the better man, we can-' started James sympathetically.

'Kiddo,' came Jared's voice from behind them both. 'It doesn't work like that. Not for people like him.' He said, nodding down to *Number One*. 'We have to end this here and now, if he goes into custody he will disappear before the sun sets.'

'So what? You want to just execute him here in the street?' scoffed James disbelievingly.

Max and Jared looked at each other, 'Yes.' They replied together. 'You will learn that sometimes the old ways are the best.' Snarled Jared.

'James,' started Max softly. 'Your father…' He turned to look James in the eye. 'This man killed your mother and father.'

James felt desperately cold, numb and suddenly breathless. All the emotion he had purposefully restricted and contained deep inside was released in an unexpected hit of pure adrenaline. He looked down at the injured old man before him. The man who had taken everything from him, who had prematurely removed his parents from the world. The man responsible for him suffering for the past three years. For turning him into what he had become. James wiped his nose with his sleeve, but his pale eyes remained dry. No more tears would be spilt, not anymore. Never again. James pulled out his pistol and steadied his breath. 'My father always told me you only live twice, once when you are born and once when you look death in the face.' He glared at the old man raising his pistol to his forehead, all hesitancy gone. 'Now you face your death.' He said coldly.

'No!' shouted Number Two walking over to them looking down at her former mentor. 'I will do it.' She said sternly. Raising her own pistol, she pointed it at the old man's cold eyes as sirens filled the air around them. Half a dozen police cars arrived as armed officers clambered out shouting and screaming at them all to get down on the ground and drop any weapons that they may be holding. These officers were not messing around.

Number Two held up a small blue warrant card above her head and unexpectantly yelled, 'Interpol!' as two officers walked towards her detaining her by the arms. 'We are executing a covert Red Notice operation; these men work for the Global Initiative Against Transnational Organized Crime.' She lowered her hands as one of the officers took and inspected her warrant card. 'Radio the Director, he will confirm our operation.' She smiled as the officer released her arm and began speaking quietly into the radio clipped to his vest as he read from her ID card. Seconds later he turned and nodded shouting to all the other officers to stand down. 'This man needs a medic.' She pointed towards Max as the officer radioed through for an ambulance.

The Dutch police officers secured the scene and minutes later the entire road was cordoned off with striped, blue police tape. Several officers stood scratching their heads looking up at the Apache helicopter wondering how they were going to recover the giant machine from the middle of the highway.

'Well?' asked Number Two to the nearest police officer. 'Have you spoken to the Director yet? We need to transfer this prisoner immediately. It is not safe to keep him on the street, he is too exposed.' She said looking around the street as if to spot an unforeseen hazard.

The officer finished with his radio; he didn't look happy. 'The Deputy Director of the Dutch Interpol office is on her way down. She wants to speak to you directly.' The officer then turned and walked to the nearest police car tapping the roof, 'Until then, he stays where he is.' Inside the vehicle *Number One* was cuffed in the back of the blue and red chevroned Netherlands Police car. He was sandwiched in the middle seat, either side of him sat a large armed response officer. Although he had remained silent, he still looked defiant, his chin up, his cold eyes glaring around at the people scurrying around outside as he observed everything, his pale lips thin and pursed tight.

*

James, Jared, Maekin and Rugen sat silently beside the pockmarked INKAS Range Rover as they watched Number Two in deep conversation with a tall olive skinned brunette in a dark trouser suit. She had arrived five minutes before and had exuded authority over the local police officers. Although the words were not audible from where they were sat, they could read both of the lady's belligerent body language. Neither backed down and it appeared neither agreed with the others suggested thoughts.

James looked over to *Number One* still sat in the rear of the Dutch police car. James could see the old man's eyes fixated on the two women standing outside his car, his thin lips began to curl into a smile. 'Is he lip reading?' he asked as he stood taking a step forward.

'What do you mean?' spat Number Two in exasperated frustration, her hands on her hips.

'We have nothing on this man.' Replied the dark trouser suit female. 'He is a ghost.' She looked over to the four sat beside the Rover, 'What I do have, is an open Yellow Notice on that young man,' she replied pointing over to James.

'This man is the head of Amsterdam office of Orion! The largest organised crime syndicate in Northern Europe.' Replied Number Two shaking her head.

'That little boy was reported missing three weeks ago in Edinburgh.' She then turned to the yellow Volkswagen Touran ambulance parked nearby where Max sat with his legs sticking out of the back seat, his trouser leg cut away as the paramedic treated his knife wound. 'He was reported missing by that man there, his uncle. Both of whom are currently showing as still being with the United Kingdom.' She turned back to Number Two, 'Can you explain this?'

Number Two just glared at the Deputy Director. Biting the side of her mouth she remained silent. 'That man is a psychopath.' She replied finally.

'Criminal psychology from a rogue agent's questionable profiling is not enough to detain someone who has never been charged with breaking the law.' Spat the Deputy Director heatedly as she turned away. 'Half of Amsterdam has been destroyed, dozens have been injured, nine people have been killed and we have eyewitnesses stating that two people from your *team* were the pilots of that stolen Apache helicopter.' The Deputy Director sucked in a large breath and puffed out her cheeks. 'So much destruction… Next thing you'll tell me is that you were involved with the massacre at the Westpoort docks.'

Number Two raised her eyebrows admittedly. 'About that…'

'Argh!' scoffed the Deputy Director walking away. 'Unbelievable.' She approached the ambulance, clicking to a nearby police officer who was standing guard. 'Arrest this man.' She pointed to Max who looked up suddenly. 'Take them all into custody and contact that man's embassy.' She said pointing to *Number One* who was now smiling broadly out of the car window. 'We will need to make a formal apology and arrange for a solicitor.' She sucked her teeth then turned back to Number Two as the officers began cuffing James, Jared, Maekin and Rugen, a new sense of trepidation visibly filled their faces.

'You!' she snapped across the main road, 'This mess is all on you.' Her phone rang as she frowned at the number displayed. She licked her lips then answered promptly, 'Yes Sir.' She nodded then turned back to Number Two. 'Yes Sir, that is right… She is here… But she has… I know that but we… When… I see…' she scowled at Number Two then hung up.

The suited female placed a hand on her forehead and closed her eyes in disbelief, 'Release them all and hand over their prisoner!' She bellowed as she walked over to Number Two glowering bitterly, 'The Director *ordered* me to send you on your way. What the hell is going on here?' She scoffed and walked away tearing the blue and white police tape down in anger as the officers then removed the handcuffs with a bewildered look.

Number One was escorted back into the INKAS Range Rover, his smile had disappeared, but his glare remained defiant. Maekin and Rugen sat either side of him and Number Two climbed into the driver's seat turning back in her seat to better view the occupants.

'Interpol?' snapped Rugen, 'Really?' she shook her head.

Number Two smiled mischievously as she pulled out her warrant card. 'Yes, Interpol, BND, CIA, Scotland Yard, GCHQ and several others.' She chuckled to herself. 'It helps to have an Ace up your sleeve.'

'And to have so many government types on your payroll.' smirked Jared climbing into the passenger seat.

'Where do you go from here Frauline?' snapped Number One.

'You know the game; you have been playing it long enough.' her tone was despondent and shallow.

'The transition of a replacement is seldom peaceful within our organisation. You think you will not be challenged?' spat Number One with a sneer.

'Challengers do not bother me; competition is more than welcome.' She turned away looking out across the sealed off crime scene to the young boy sat with his injured uncle who was still being tended to by the paramedic. 'What concerns me,' she continued turning back to Number One. 'Is what you may have playing out as we speak. What ulterior motives and chaos you may have instored for us all.'

Number One just lifted his head and laughed to himself. He lowered his head licking his lips as he leant in closer to Number Two. 'You expect me to just sit back and let you take *My* empire from me?'

'Orion was built to stop all organised crime, to put an end to people's suffering,' scoffed Number Two, but Number One just shook his head despondently.

'Backing from all of the major governments gave us unrestricted access into the heart of this world.' He smiled, raising his handcuffed hands open palmed. 'We are top of the food chain, leaders in the entire market and you want to throw all of this away for your naive mentality of a good cause.' His face displayed an utter disgust as if he had inhaled a foul smell.

'We communicate with these government agencies so that we can gain the advantage over the underworld leaders. We pass them information and in return they pass us the information that we need to stop tyrants like Chen.'

'Finally, something that I agree upon,' sneered Number One wagging his finger, before touching his ear. 'Communication is an absolute must.' He laughed maniacally once more as he looked around at his former associates sitting either side of him and before him.

Number Two glared at him but as he turned she could just make out a tiny silica dot inside Number One's ear canal. 'Scheisse!' she called as he elbowed Maekin hard in the mouth sending him back against the seats headrest. Rugen threw a punch at him, but he easily blocked it with one hand using his free hand to grab her fingers. A hideous snap filled the back seat as Rugen shrieked an agonising tone. Her bruised eyes watched in terror as she saw three of her fingers folding backwards over her knuckles as they popped out of their sockets. Maekin shook his head touching at his bloodied nose as he turned back to Number One with a malicious glare within his eyes. He grabbed the old man and squeezed him violently around the neck as the old man wheezed out an agonising breath. Rugen sat back against the vehicle window and kicked the old man hard in the face with her heel. Simultaneously Maekin applied more pressure as the old man gasped, his old lips turning blue, and his eyes turned bloodshot and red. Sweat appeared on his scarred forehead as he wriggled helplessly to rid himself of the hulk that was Maekin.

Outside of the vehicle the sound of screeching tyres filled the otherwise silent streets. Number Two and Jared exchanged a look as three vans appeared around the stationary police cars; one van pushed a police car aside as it continued towards their parked Range Rover.

Number Two started the engine and pulled out her pistol, throwing it at Jared. 'We need to secure him, we have to find out what else he has set in motion. He may be the only one who can stop it.' she spat as she revved the four-litre engine pulling the gear stick out of neutral. Jared nodded and ejected the pistol magazine spinning in his seat. Without so much of a word he pistol-whipped Number One across the face, subduing him instantly as Maekin released the pressure with a look of disappointment across his face.

Their Range Rover sped off as the first van arrived just behind them, inches from making a hideous impact with their rear bumper. The Dutch police still on scene stood agog as the three transporter vans began to pursue the bullet scarred Range Rover. Hitting 150 kmph in only eight seconds they reached the end of the dual carriageway that led onto the large motorway heading north. As the roads opened up and widened she slipped the large vehicle down to fifth then back up into sixth gear flooring the pedal taking it up to 230 kmph. Unlike most Range Rovers that have eight speed gears the heavier armoured INKAS only had six, but for something that weighed over a tonne it sure could move. Her arms were visibly tense under her short-sleeved blouse as she threw the beast of the vehicle around slower traffic. For a mature woman she had a well-defined and muscular body and this drive was making use of each and every muscle she had.

They were all thrown forward in their seats as the chasing Mercedes-Benz Transporter van rammed them aggressively. Turning to Jared she spoke calmly and authoritatively, 'Lose them Monsieur Araignée.' she huffed as she swerved around a large lorry as their perusing vans cascade drove in a serpentine motion quickly behind them.

Jared removed his side arm as he lowered the passenger window, Number Two placed a hand on his thigh, 'I think this will be more effective.' she smiled leaning over to the glove box, snapping it open she pulled out a small green pineapple shaped fragmentation grenade before handing over to Jared.

Jared raised an eyebrow but took the with a simple nod as he turned in his seat to stalk the van. It did not take much as he could see the van driver directly behind them. 'When I say, slam on the brake then speed up...' he shouted as he pulled the safety pin out releasing the safety lever, counting silently in his head he shouted, 'Now!!' as Number Two slammed her foot down on the brake pedal. The chasing van crunched into the back of them, but all the damage was transferred and absorbed by the chasing Transporter, the bonnet and grill had been crumpled inwards and the bumper now dragged along the motorway creating small sparks as the vehicle slowed momentarily from the blunt force impact of the collision. Number One's unconscious body lurched forward between the drivers and passengers' seat as Jared skilfully dropped the grenade in a half throw behind them as it rattled along the tarmac.

The vans front wheel had just gone over the small explosive as a sickening pop was followed by a violent bang rang out as the vans front tyres exploded outwards from the fragmentation and shrapnel within the grenade. The van driver looked horrified in the split second he had before his seat and all of the front cab of the Mercedes van became engulfed in a sudden orangey-yellow ball of flame. Jared watched in the rear-view mirror as the now wheelless van dropped down and squealed to an agonising halt as the buckled chassis and ravaged and twisted flaming body acted as a brake against the dark asphalt.

The Range Rover shot away as the two remaining Transporter vans careened around their fallen companion continuing their chase, the occupants now opening fire on the Range Rover. The first few rounds pinged off the reinforced glass with very little effect. Jared replied with several shots out of his window as he watched one of the drivers throw his empty pistol back inside his window only to reach over and pick up a small but chunky snub nose revolver. Jared squinted to see what the man was doing but he soon realised and pulled his head back inside the Range Rover. 'Get your blerrie heads down!' he hollered as the entire rear window exploded into a shower of tiny glass fragments.

Jared stayed low in his seat as he spoke, 'He has a Taurus Judge Revolver, this thing can take down a blerrie Kodiak bear at fifty yards.'

This cheap but extremely powerful Brazilian revolver was like any normal five chamber cylinder pistol, but this one had been adapted by Orion. The extra-long cylinder allowed the user to fire a .45 Long Colt cartridge or a 2.5-inch .410 bore shotshell load. This specific revolver was loaded with high-explosive armour piercing cartridges, a favourite for Orion agents due to its compact size and devastating power.

Another round exploded just inside the boot of the Range Rover blowing out the remaining glass and windows at the rear of the vehicle just behind Rugen's headrest. The blast from the explosion still rang within all of their ears making it impossible to hear what was being said. Jared looked across to Number Two who was shouting at him, but the only sound he could hear was the constant disorientating ringing that filled his entire head. He looked to the back seats to find Maekin was relentlessly firing over the top of the seat at the hounding vans just behind them. Beside him Number One lay still, his head forward not moving. Further across the back seat he saw Rugen, and his heart suddenly sank. He tried to reach across to grab her wrist to check for a pulse, but he couldn't quite make it without allowing the van drivers a clear shot of his torso. Rugen sat upright in her seat, her head back and eyes rolled up staring at the pockmarked and burnt leather ceiling. Blood trickled out of her open mouth, but her body was completely still. Number Two swerved around another freighter lorry rocking the occupant's side to side as Rugen's body then fell silently forward. Jared could see that the last explosive round had blown away half of the back of her head. The rear passenger side door suddenly became engulfed in flame as a huge hole blew out the armoured metal work.

'The car can't take much more of this.' shouted Number Two to Jared's surprise he could now hear her again, but she was still very muffled and muted, 'The Apache caused too much structural damage. We need to get off the road and lose them.' She called, pointing a thumb over her shoulder as she swerved more traffic.

'The Apache…' thought Jared, he pulled out his mobile phone and hit dial. 'Kiddo, tell Max we could use a little help out here.'

'I will see what I can do.' Shouted James. 'Where are you?'

'Just follow the smoke.' Smiled Jared, hanging up the phone.

'I am out!' snapped Maekin from behind them dropping his empty pistol, it was no longer of any use to him. He turned back to face the others, he paused on seeing Rugen sat across from him but remained silent. He knew the cost of this game. 'Do we have any more weapons?' he said sniffing hard as another explosion went off outside the vehicle. This blast was absorbed by the armoured door but still knocked them sideways several feet causing Number Two to grip the steering wheel even tighter.

Jared shook his head holding up his own empty pistol, Number Two remained focused on the road, the traffic had begun to slow as tailbacks formed ahead of them amongst a sea of glowing red lights. Maekin sighed and leant across to search his dead friend's body. He pulled out a small knife and one magazine clip. 'Only eight rounds...' shouted Maekin, his hearing still not 100%.

He reloaded Rugen's dropped pistol and sat with both arms over the headrest. He took time to train the sight on the driver with the Taurus revolver, two short successive snaps later and the driver slumped over the steering wheel ploughing into the central reservation at excessive speed. The second van drove right up to the Range Rover's bumper ramming several times as it released several blasts through the broken window.

'To hell with this!' shouted Maekin as he climbed over the headrests into the exposed boot space. Even though he was a bear of a man he still looked small in the expanse of the vehicle's huge trunk. The Mercedes van approached for another ram as Maekin simultaneously climbed out of the rear window letting off three shots through the van's windscreen, shattering it. What he did next surprised not only the van driver but also his two companions in the front of the Range Rover. With a guttural roar he leapt out of the trunk and into the passenger seat of the van grabbing the driver's long hair in a large fist with one hand. His other hand gripped Rugen's pistol as he held it to the temple of the startled driver as he released the remaining three bullets through the man's head at point blank range. Pulling the cadaver out of the driver's seat Maekin slowed the van before pulling alongside the Range Rover. 'If we do not make it out of this alive, I want you to know I liked you.' he smiled, shouting through the Transporter van's shattered windscreen to Jared and Number Two.

The traffic ahead had now stopped completely as the two battle scarred vehicles rolled to a crawl side by side. People were seen running back along the motorway in sheer panic as Jared tried to see what was obstructing the motorway up ahead, then he saw it and instantly wished he hadn't. His jaw dropped as he saw a mottled green, brown and black Dutch Leopard 2A6 tank sitting half a mile further up the carriage way in the middle of the live lane. 'Stop!' he exclaimed, 'Stop the blerrie car-!'

"Boom!"

Number Two was pulled out by Maekin who had already decamped the van. Jared was already over the central reservation as the Range Rover disintegrated before their eyes. A small heap of twisted black charred metal now sat where their armoured vehicle had just been as thick dark smoke billowed up into the otherwise beautiful blue summer sky. Jared climbed back to his feet rubbing his aching body as his old stitches began to weep through his top. He connected eyes with Maekin and Number Two who were on the other side of the wreckage as they looked agog at the detritus shell that lay before them. 'Did you get Number One out?' shouted Number Two from across the three lanes. Jared shook his head looking into the smouldering fiery heap of metal, nothing had survived the impact.

The tanks Rheinmetall 120 mm smoothbore L/55 gun bellowed for a second time as the Mercedes van peeled open as if it were made of cheap aluminium foil. The impact sent it back twenty feet as they all hit the decks once more. Jared could see the glint of a reflection from the panoramic PERI R17 sight spinning left to right as the tank driver searched for its target, which ultimately was them. The gun's accuracy and devastating power made him wish he wasn't now wearing a bright yellow hoodie.

'Jared!' shouted Number Two as she frantically pointed towards the tank.

'Yes...' he snapped, 'I have seen it.' he replied frustratedly, shaking his head.

'No, you fool, look!' she shouted sternly. Jared rose his head ever so slightly just to see past the front dozen cars to see a limping figure of a man with bound hands sprinting towards the waiting tank. It was Number One. Unbelievably, he had somehow managed to climb out of the Range Rover seconds before the tank had annihilated it and then run straight past them as they took cover.

'We must stop him, at any cost... Even if it means losing all of our lives.' called Number Two.

Jared looked around for some inspiration, *"No vehicle, no weapons, no ideas of how to stop a super tank"* he smacked his forehead on finding no inspiration. He tried calling Max on his phone put it rang out to voicemail. Puffing his cheeks defeatedly he manoeuvred in a squatted walk over to join the others, 'Give me the knife.' He told Maekin, his hand outstretched.

'But that is all we have to fight with...' protested Maekin, like a scolded child losing a favourite toy. He huffed as he handed it over reluctantly.

'We need to stop him before he reaches that tank, or we would have failed, and all of this would have been for nothing.' snapped Number Two angrily.

'Maybe we can split up and try and get behind it?' asked Maekin with a shrug.

'The turret can turn a full 360 degrees in 9 seconds, it will be on us before we even make it halfway or within twenty metres of it.' hissed Jared rubbing his jaw. 'Live today, die tomorrow, right?' he half smiled as he began sprinting after Number One.

Using the stationary cars as cover Jared moved quickly and silently as he gained on the limping figure of Number One. His confidence shattered when he heard another deafening boom from in front of him. Swearing he dove sideways and kept rolling until he was on the gravel verge beneath the central reservation barrier. The vehicle he had just been squatting behind lifted ten feet off the ground and burst like a firework mid-air sending car parts, glass and shrapnel everywhere before it crashed back down with a gut-wrenching crunching tang of metal on tarmac.

Jared jumped back up to his feet, *"No point in hiding now they knew he was there, right?"* he asked himself, brushing down the gravel, glass and unidentifiable cack that frequented the side of motorways. He moved quickly as he saw Number One gaining on the tank, now only one hundred metres away. He had to dive several times as more vehicles exploded from the shell fire of the Leopard 2A6 as they tried to impede his approach, but they were not as quick as him. Using larger vehicles as cover, he managed to come within ten metres of Number One. He was so close, but he knew it would not be long until the tank crew opened the hatch and popped up with machine guns and all other kinds of surprises for him. He had to end this now, and quickly. Grinding his teeth, he sucked in as much air as he could then sprinted with everything he had left inside his broken, bruised and exhausted body towards Number One. The old man's limp meant that he was slow and made him stumble several times making the journey very uncomfortable and agonising on his already injured legs. Jared was now only four metres away when he saw the hatch lift open on the tank sitting only fifty metres ahead of them. He had to act now.

Pulling out Rugen's knife he squeezed the handle and paused, controlling his breath he tried to stop his hands from shaking. His adrenaline was all he had left to work with, the fatigue would have knocked a normal man out an hour ago, but Jared kept on going. He raised the knife high above his shoulder and charged forward with all the strength he could muster. He drove the knife down hard making contact with the old man's thigh. One final movement, maximum effort.

The knife found its target and the blade sank in up to the hilt knocking the old man to the floor with a cry of pain and fear as he hugged his mauled leg. Jared smiled as the old man squirmed on the floor not able to stand up. The tank's open hatch was now sporting a dark, sallow-skinned man holding a large scoped assault rifle. He lowered the rifle menacingly, training it on Jared, his finger on the trigger. Jared stood defiant, head held high and shoulders although heaving from exhaustion were held back with pride. He raised his middle finger to the tank man and was about to shout the obscenest insult he could think of, knowing this was his final stand. The last few seconds of his crazy life. When the man in the tank squealed and ducked back inside the tank. 'What the-' he spun on his heels to see the battered Apache rushing towards him only feet above the roofs of the stationary vehicles. There in the pilot's and co-pilot's seats were Max and James Bond.

The Apache released three successive HellFire missiles at the tank before it banked hard to the left preempting a counter strike from the occupants of the Leopard. Jared watched as the three, five-foot long missiles shot over his head towards the tank. The long barrel of the Leopard rose thirty degrees, but it was simply too late. Jared was thrown backwards from the impact blast and into the windscreen of a nearby family saloon car as the huge tank erupted in a cacophony of bangs, thuds and blasts as the entire machine contorted and twisted as each missile found its target perfectly.

*

Jared woke to find James, two fire crew and a beautiful paramedic lifting him out of the family saloon's crushed windscreen. His mouth and nose were covered with a transparent oxygen mask, and he noticed he had a tube sticking out of his left wrist attached to a bag of clear liquid being held by one of the fire crew. He suddenly realised that they must have given him something for the pain as he felt positively euphoric and somewhat giddy.

'We did it,' said James with a smile.

'Your father would be proud of you kiddo.' Whispered Jared through the oxygen mask. His words slightly muffled. 'You give everything, you get the job done no matter what the cost.' He winced as the paramedic tightened the strap on the board stretcher as he was lifted down to a waiting rolling collapsible wheeled gurney. 'Reputation is one thing, but actions are what really matter.' He closed his tired eyes as the medicine took hold of him.

Number Two was stood by another stretcher where Maekin was being prodded and poked by some more paramedics, he clearly didn't like the fuss and kept telling them to leave him alone. She saw Jared being lifted down onto his own stretcher as she walked over beside him taking his tube free hand. 'Danke Jared.' she whispered. He felt her squeezing his hand, but he couldn't respond. The tiredness, painkillers and the oxygen mask made it almost impossible, so he nodded gently and once again closed his eyes.

When he opened them again, he was inside a hospital room, the room looked private by the décor and high-end equipment that he was attached to. On one of the walls a large LCD television was showing aerial shots from the news helicopters of the motorway and the carnage that had played out there. He looked to his side to see James sat eating some grapes and Max sat beside him in a wheelchair. James placed the grapes beside the table that was adorned with "Get well soon" cards and stood up. James honestly didn't know who they could have been from considering the lifestyle Jared lived. *"I suppose drug dealers, coffee shop and gun shop owners and backstreet doctors are humans too."* He shrugged to himself as he smiled at Jared's bruised face.

'You've been out for hours.' boomed Max from his wheelchair. 'They said it was a wee miracle that you even made it, considering the amount of blood you'd lost. And the internal organ damage... and the spinal injury.' Jared raised a hand to stop him talking. Even with all the painkillers Max's booming voice was too much for his tired head.

James laughed, 'We are just glad you are alright.'

Jared lifted his head to drink some water before wincing from his bruised ribs. 'So, did we win kiddo?'

James nodded soberly, 'Number One is under investigation by the Hague. Number Two is somewhere.' He shrugged with a laugh. 'I don't think her battle is quite over yet.' He looked seriously at Jared who nodded back.

'Orion has all but officially been decommissioned, in Amsterdam at least. I am afraid you may now be out of a job.' Said Max.

'So I can look forward to some peace and blerrie quiet?' laughed Jared.

'For now...' said Max soberly, 'But we all know how there will never be an *end* to this lifestyle. Dictators are replaced, countries are redesignated, regimes are renamed, and new crime syndicates just supplant the previous one.' His tone was earnest, subdued and staidly.

'Like the Lernaean Hydra. You cut one head off and two more grow back.' answered James.

'Exactly James.' replied Max.

'The boy learns fast Max...' started Jared unpretentiously. 'Although, I feel he needs a proper teacher. And a more sedate role model. Someone more circumspect in their daily pursuits.' he laughed and regretted it immediately. The pain was terrible.

'Out of harm's way...' nodded Max, placing a hand on James' shoulder. 'James, I feel it is time to take you back home.'

'Uncle, I appreciate that, but I am not cut out for that school.' James protested heartedly.

'No James...' he paused for a moment then smiled again. 'Home to Skyfall.' James stood silent as he watched his uncle's eyes well up. 'It is time. For both of us.'

James nodded and closed his eyes. 'I came here to find myself.' He said turning to them both in turn, 'And I can honestly say that what I found within me was a part of you Max, and you Jared, and my father. Now I am ready for my next adventure.'

'It's been a blast kiddo.' smiled Jared shaking the boy's hand, 'If you are ever in Amsterdam...' he nodded without finishing the sentence. James thanked him for everything and walked to the door as a young nurse entered.

'You never know Jared,' smiled Max immaturely, 'You may be getting a bed bath.' He turned to the young nurse and smiled at her. 'Let's see if you can guess why they call him Monsieur Araignée.'

'Monsieur Araignée?' asked the nurse, perplexed.

'You'll see.' they all laughed as they closed the door behind them.

*

James and Max were escorted to a private area within the Amsterdam ferry port. A small ramp led down to a slimy seldom used slipway that lowered into the sea. Beside that was a narrow aluminum and steel gangway of rusted steps. At the bottom of this waited a high-powered Fast Response Targa 31 patrol boat.

'You know James...' started Max seriously, 'I have an old friend who works at the University of Geneva, Switzerland. Do you ken that's near to where you learned to ski with your mother all those years ago. That little resort in Kitzbuhel.' James's cheeks reddened at the mention of his mother, 'I only mention it because of the Universities motto, *Post tenebras lux*. Light after darkness. I think it is quite fitting.' His uncle looked out over the sea as his eyes welled up. 'You mind giving it a wee thought, during the crossing back home... It would mean the world to your aunty Charmian and me that you finished your education.'

Max went on first and shook hands with the heavily armed Clandestine Channel Threat Commander who had been sent on behalf of the British Home Office to bring them back to England. The two of them spoke in almost silence for a moment before the officer approached James who was still standing on terra firma.

The young Naval officer offered his hand. 'I am Commander Fleming of the Home Office's Clandestine-'

'I know who you are sir. My uncle has told me all about the two of you and your history.' smiled James, taking the proffered hand firmly. 'Pleased to meet you.'

The Commander smiled; his face was charming yet weathered at the same time and his eyes were sharp and observant. 'You know you gave us all quite the surprise when we heard about your exploits and illegal voyage across the North Sea.' James stood in silence not knowing just how much trouble he was in. The Commander read the boy's nervous body language and climbed up so one foot remained on the harbour wall and one firmly on the boat's low gunwale. 'No need to be anxious.' He smiled again, 'We are all very impressed.' His demeanour was very reassuring and somehow James immediately felt at ease around the man. He couldn't put his finger on it, but he somewhat reminded him of Jared. That same cocky yet cunning attitude, his diabolical yet debonair charm and high intellect. James had an instant affinity with this man. *"Role model material"* he thought to himself with a smile.

'You have some unique talents young man...' he said, holding his shoulder, helping him off the harbour wall and onto the bow of the high-powered Fast Response Targa 31 patrol boat. 'These talents can be harnessed and perfected to a deadly proficiency. Have you ever thought about joining the Royal Navy Reserve?' he raised an eyebrow and looked over to the armed response officers standing behind them. 'We need people like you, Mr?'

'Bond, James Bond.'

The End

Printed in Great Britain
by Amazon

14956653R00099